"There's something I have to show you."

Alison handed Brady the envelope and said, "This might come as a shock."

Brady frowned and opened the envelope, his hands shaking as he pulled out the marriage certificate—their marriage certificate. Then he removed the next set of papers and his eyes met hers.

"They're our annulment papers," Alison said in a low voice. "My grandmother sent them to me in my hope chest."

"But they haven't been processed. What's going on?"

"Apparently Dad asked Grammy Rose to file them and she…forgot."

It took just a second for him to realize the implications. "Then…we're…"

"That's right, Brady. We're still married."

Dear Reader,

Heartwarming, emotional, compelling…these are all words that describe Harlequin American Romance. Check out this month's stellar selection of love stories, which are sure to delight you.

First, Debbi Rawlins delivers the exciting conclusion of Harlequin American Romance's continuity series, TEXAS SHEIKHS. In *His Royal Prize*, sparks fly immediately between dashing sheikh Sharif and Desert Rose ranch hand Olivia Smith. However, Sharif never expected their romantic tryst to be plastered all over the tabloids—or that the only way to salvage their reputations would be to make Olivia his royal bride.

Bestselling author Muriel Jensen pens another spectacular story in her WHO'S THE DADDY? miniseries with *Daddy To Be Determined*, in which a single gal's ticking biological clock leads her to convince a single dad that he's the perfect man to father her baby. In *Have Husband, Need Honeymoon*, the third book in Rita Herron's THE HARTWELL HOPE CHESTS miniseries, Alison Hartwell thought her youthful marriage to an air force pilot had been annulled, but surprise! Now a forced reunion with her "husband" has her wondering if a second honeymoon couldn't give them a second chance at forever. And Harlequin American Romance's promotion THE WAY WE MET…AND MARRIED continues with *The Best Blind Date in Texas*. Don't miss this wonderful romance from Victoria Chancellor.

It's a great lineup, and we hope you enjoy them all!

Wishing you happy reading,

Melissa Jeglinski
Associate Senior Editor
Harlequin American Romance

HAVE HUSBAND, NEED HONEYMOON
Rita Herron

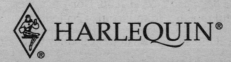

TORONTO • NEW YORK • LONDON
AMSTERDAM • PARIS • SYDNEY • HAMBURG
STOCKHOLM • ATHENS • TOKYO • MILAN • MADRID
PRAGUE • WARSAW • BUDAPEST • AUCKLAND

To Melissa Endlich—
Thanks for helping me give life to this one.
I hope it's the first of many more books we do together!

ISBN 0-373-16883-7

HAVE HUSBAND, NEED HONEYMOON

Copyright © 2001 by Rita B. Herron.

All rights reserved. Except for use in any review, the reproduction or
utilization of this work in whole or in part in any form by any electronic,
mechanical or other means, now known or hereafter invented, including
xerography, photocopying and recording, or in any information storage
or retrieval system, is forbidden without the written permission of the
publisher, Harlequin Enterprises Limited, 225 Duncan Mill Road,
Don Mills, Ontario, Canada M3B 3K9.

All characters in this book have no existence outside the imagination of
the author and have no relation whatsoever to anyone bearing the same
name or names. They are not even distantly inspired by any individual
known or unknown to the author, and all incidents are pure invention.

This edition published by arrangement with Harlequin Books S.A.

® and TM are trademarks of the publisher. Trademarks indicated with
® are registered in the United States Patent and Trademark Office, the
Canadian Trade Marks Office and in other countries.

Visit us at www.eHarlequin.com

Printed in U.S.A.

ABOUT THE AUTHOR

Rita Herron is a teacher, workshop leader and storyteller who loves reading, writing and sharing stories with people of all ages. She has published two nonfiction books for adults on working and playing with children, and has won the Golden Heart award for a young adult story. Rita believes that books taught her to dream, and she loves nothing better than sharing that magic with others. She lives with her "dream" husband and three children, two cats and a dog in Norcross, Georgia.

Books by Rita Herron

HARLEQUIN AMERICAN ROMANCE

HARLEQUIN INTRIGUE

Don't miss any of our special offers. Write to us at the following address for information on our newest releases.

Harlequin Reader Service
U.S.: 3010 Walden Ave., P.O. Box 1325, Buffalo, NY 14269
Canadian: P.O. Box 609, Fort Erie, Ont. L2A 5X3

LETTER FROM GRANDMOTHER

My sweet, darling Alison,

You've always been a special granddaughter to me because you are the last link to our past, the last link to our future. Endings are usually sad, but you taught us that endings can also be a joy.

You readily accepted the broken toys, the hand-me-down clothes, the hectic life and schedule of a single father. You were always sensitive to others, the peacemaker between your sisters during their turbulent years, always the one to hold the family together. You have the rare gift of knowing when to listen as well as talk, and you touch everything in life with wisdom and kindness. When we tried to baby you, you fought for independence and won. But even when your hair turns gray like mine and your children grow taller than you, you will still be my baby.

I hope you learn to speak your mind, to sometimes rock the boat without worrying about what others might think. I wish for you happiness, true love and a man that will be your equal and bring you all the joy a partner can.

Love you always,

Grammy Rose

Chapter One

"Thomas asked me to marry him."

Still glowing from their own recent weddings, Mimi and Hannah, Alison Hartwell's two older sisters, exchanged odd looks.

Alison had expected them to jump up and down and start making plans right away, so their lack of exuberance surprised her, especially since they were sitting in the middle of her bridal shop, Weddings to Remember. Every time they gathered here, they talked about weddings. Hannah's wedding to Jake Tippins, a sexy cop who'd almost arrested their father. Mimi's wedding to Hannah's ex-fiancé, Seth Broadhurst. The fact that Hannah had fixed Alison up with the handsome obstetrician gynecologist the minute he'd driven into town. The fact that Alison had caught the bouquet at Mimi's wedding. The hope chests their grandmother Rose had sent them that had seemingly been a catalyst for choosing their mates—and for the craziness in their lives.

"That's great," levelheaded Hannah finally said. "Thomas is a wonderful doctor."

Mimi, folded hands across the bulging mound of

her pregnant belly, kicked off her shoes to reveal swollen ankles. "Yeah, he has a good sense of humor."

Hannah straightened the stack of bridal magazines on the round table between them. "And all his women patients love him." She frowned. "I don't mean they're in love with him, I—"

"I know what you mean," Alison said.

"He *is* an OB-GYN." Mimi wrinkled her nose. "Let's hope his women patients love him. After all, he doesn't have *men* patients."

Mimi laughed at her own joke, and Alison and Hannah both shook their heads.

"Come to think of it," Mimi continued, "marrying a gynecologist would be kind of weird. Do you think he ever gets tired of—"

"I'm sure he gets tired of that *question*," Hannah said, cutting her off.

Mimi giggled mischievously and grabbed Alison's hand, checking her third finger. "No ring, huh? What is he, cheap or something?"

Hannah frowned at Mimi. "So what did you tell him, Ali?"

Alison picked up a piece of baby's breath and brought it to her nose, inhaling the sweet scent. She loved all the smells in her shop—the lilac-scented spray she used to lighten the air, the fresh flowers in the entryway, the potpourri in the crystal dish beside the display of bridal books. "I haven't given him an answer yet."

Hannah's blond eyebrows rose. "But you're considering his proposal?"

"I told him I needed time to think about it."

Mimi nodded, her rosy lips pursed. "Not sure he's the one?"

"Mimi!" Hannah chided.

"Well, he's rushing it, isn't he? You two have only been dating a couple of months," Mimi said.

"This coming from you?" Alison asked dryly. "The woman who went from thinking Seth was boring to a torrid affair in a matter of hours?"

They both glanced at Mimi's belly. Mimi grinned, a wicked glint in her eyes. "Okay, well, sometimes being in a hurry isn't so bad."

Hannah stood, shaking her head at Mimi. "Sorry, girls, I have to get back to the clinic."

"And I have to meet Seth at the coffee shop. He's bringing a group over for role playing in the Book Nook section." Mimi struggled to pull her bulky weight up from the chair, accepting Hannah's outstretched hand with a sigh. "I guess I could play a whale or an elephant if they need one."

Alison chuckled. "Don't be silly, you look great."

"Yeah, you're the prettiest whale we know," Hannah said, patting Mimi's back.

Mimi rolled her eyes and smiled. "Just wait, payback will be fun, sis."

"Hannah, are you—"

"No," Hannah said softly, a sheepish look on her face. "But someday. We're having too much fun together right now."

They all laughed, and Alison pointed to a large box in the corner. "I'd better get busy, too. I need to unpack that shipment before Vivica drops by to discuss her wedding."

"Oh, by the way, how's her brother, Brady?" Hannah asked. "He was in the Air Force, right?"

"Yeah."

"You used to have a thing for him, didn't you?" Mimi asked.

"That was a long time ago," Alison said.

"Is he coming for Vivica's wedding?" Hannah asked.

Alison shrugged. "I don't know."

Hannah's beeper zinged and she checked the number. "Now I really have to go." She tucked a strand of Alison's hair behind her ear, her big sister role firmly in place. "Take your time thinking about the proposal, sis. I like Thomas a lot, but don't let him push you into something you're not ready for."

"Yeah, he's got to be the one that lights your fire and keeps it burning all night long," Mimi added.

Would Thomas do that? Alison wondered. So far, she hadn't felt that animal magnetism. When Hannah had first described him, she'd expected him to knock her socks off with sex appeal, but instead he'd sort of tickled her socked toes with his nice friendly smile. Still, their friendship would make for a good stable marriage, she rationalized. And she was ready to settle down.

Instantly Brady Broussard's face rose in her mind. Her body automatically tingled, bittersweet memories assaulting her. The dates in high school. The prom. The night they'd secretly gotten married. Brady had certainly made her burn all night, like dancing the mambo instead of a waltz. And in spite of the immediate annulment her father had insisted upon, Brady had kept the embers hot for three years with his romantic letters and promises to return. But the fourth year he'd suddenly stopped writing, and it had been like cold water dousing the fire. He'd broken her heart so badly she'd thought she'd never recover.

Hannah smiled slyly. "This is one time I agree with Mimi. Friendship's nice, but the sparks are important, too."

"You two are so mushy about those husbands of yours it's unbelievable."

Alison hugged them both and tried to banish thoughts of Brady from her mind. Maybe Thomas would help her forget him. So what if fireworks didn't explode when he kissed her? The pain wouldn't be so bad if things didn't work out. She'd only been thinking about Brady because she was coordinating his sister's wedding. Not because she was still in love with the man.

No, Thomas was a great guy—fun, easygoing. And he and Vivica's fiancé were best friends, so the four of them could double date.

"You don't want to tell him yes, then run from the altar like Hannah did." Mimi dragged Hannah toward the door. "Of course, I wouldn't have a husband right now if Hannah hadn't jilted Seth." The girls laughed again and Alison waved them off.

A few minutes later, Alison stared at the contents of the crate, a mixture of awe and apprehension engulfing her. When she'd caught the bouquet at Mimi's wedding, she'd whispered to her grandmother, telling her about Thomas's proposal.

Now her hope chest had arrived.

Her Grammy Rose was probably already pruning

the flowers around the gazebo for the wedding, and Alison hadn't even accepted Thomas's proposal!

She ran her hand over the hope chest, her heart fluttering. It was a beautiful, gold-embossed chest with intricate hearts carved on the outside, similar but slightly different in design from Hannah's and Mimi's. When Hannah and Mimi had received their chests, their lives had spun topsy-turvy out of control.

Alison's fingers trembled as she unfastened the latch.

Would her life do the same?

BRADY BROUSSARD SETTLED into his assigned seat on Flight 1213, rubbed his throbbing leg and tried to straighten it in front of him in the narrow space, then punched his sister's number on his cell phone while he waited for the other passengers to board. Vivica's phone rang twice, then she answered in her normally cheerful voice.

"Vivica here."

"Hey, sis, it's me."

"Brady! How are you feeling? Where are you? Are you on your way?"

"Whoa, slow down." He chuckled, feeling his throat thicken with emotion. Thank God for Vivica; he hadn't realized how much he needed her until now. And not just for the physical therapy she'd promised to help him with. "I'm okay. I made the flight to Washington. I'll spend the night there, then fly home tomorrow."

"Super! You'll be here in time for the parade!"

Oh, hell. He'd been gone from Sugar Hill so long he'd forgotten about the big Fourth of July festivities. He didn't want to disappoint Vivica, but he didn't intend on joining the activities. Sugar Hill always celebrated with a parade, crafts for the kids, pony rides and fireworks.

Fireworks reminded him of Alison Hartwell and that incredibly erotic night by the lake. The last time he'd seen her. The one night she'd spent with him as his wife. No, he wasn't up for a parade and a trip down memory lane. He was a different man now. "I'm not sure I'll make it in time, sis."

"Oh, Brady, please try—"

"Look, Vivi, I'm coming home to recuperate, not to socialize." His hand automatically went to his pocket, where he still kept two of Alison's letters.

She was the only woman he'd ever loved or wanted.

But he wasn't the same man he'd been when he'd left Sugar Hill years ago. He never would be again.

"No, Brady, *you* look. All your old friends will want to see you. You haven't been back since you joined the Air Force, and that's been almost four years."

"I know." After his father's death, he'd hated coming home. And Alison had been away at school anyway. He wouldn't be back now if he hadn't been injured in a recent crash and been forced to take a medical leave to recover from the wounds. But his best friend had died right next to him. He wasn't sure he'd ever recover.

Because he was partly at fault.

"Just promise me you won't tell Mom I'm coming. I don't want her making a big deal out of my arrival. We're going to focus on your wedding."

"All right, all right. As a matter of fact, I'm on my way to see the wedding coordinator now. I'm so glad you'll be here to run interference between me and Mom."

"How is she?"

"Being her usual self." Vivica sighed. "She means well, but I want a simple wedding and I'm afraid she'll let things get out of hand."

Their mother could be pushy. After their father's funeral, she'd pressured Brady to take over his father's print shop, not join the Air Force. But he'd refused because he'd been gung ho to be a fighter pilot like his dad had been in his early years.

Now Brady didn't know what he was going to do with his life.

Vivica was chattering away about her wedding plans, something about whether or not to invite their great-aunt Bernadette, who had a penchant for pickpocketing, and he tried to focus. He was glad Vivica had found happiness.

"I can't wait to meet this guy," Brady said. "He'd better be good to you. I'd hate to have to beat him up. I learned some pretty good moves in training." Only he was too out of shape to use them.

Vivica laughed and assured him he'd like Joe. Then Brady hung up. He had to get some sleep. He just prayed that this time when he fell asleep, the nightmares of the accident wouldn't return to haunt him.

ALISON SLOWLY UNFASTENED the latch to the hope chest and peeked inside. A pale gold envelope sat on top of mounds of gold tissue. She pulled out the stationery and smiled at her grandmother's loopy handwriting.

My sweet, darling Alison,
You've always been a special granddaughter to me because you are the last link to our past, the last link to our future. Endings are usually sad, but you taught us that endings can also be a joy.

You readily accepted the broken toys, the hand-me-down clothes, the hectic life and schedule of a single father. You were always sensitive to others, the peacemaker between your sisters during their turbulent years, always the one to hold the family together. You have the rare gift of knowing when to listen as well as talk, and you touch everything in life with wisdom and kindness. When we tried to baby you, you fought for independence and won. But even when your hair turns gray like mine and your children grow taller than you, you will still be my baby.

I hope you learn to speak your mind, to sometimes rock the boat without worrying about what others might think. I wish for you happiness, true love and a man who will be your equal and bring you all the joy a partner can.

Love you always,
Grammy Rose

Alison wiped a tear from the corner of her eye and removed the top layer of tissue paper, her breath catching at the sight of her grandmother's bridal veil. She recognized it from Grammy Rose's wedding pictures; the narrow tiara with ivory porcelain roses and pearl-and-rhinestone accents gave way to yards and yards of sheer white netting that would cascade down the bride's back in exquisite, billowing folds. Excited, Alison pulled away more tissue and discovered a new pair of white satin gloves, beaded with pearls and rhinestones almost identical to the ones on the veil. A lacy blue garter lay beside it. Something old, something new, something borrowed, something blue.

Digging deeper, she uncovered an envelope and an eight-by-ten, ivory porcelain picture frame with wedding bells etched on the side. Then she flipped the frame over and gasped. A picture of her and Brady stared back at her—the photo of the two of them the night they'd gotten married.

The memory of that crazy wonderful night and the three months before flashed back in painful clarity.

On prom night, they'd been hot in love, hadn't been able to keep their hands off each other. One thing led to another and they'd given in to their passion and made love out by the lake. Their feelings had escalated over the summer. Brady had promised he'd love her forever, and had begged her to marry him. In a frenzy of emotions, mostly desperation that they would soon be parting, they'd sneaked away and gotten a marriage license. The night before he was to leave for the Air Force, they'd woken up a local preacher and had married at midnight in the little chapel by the lake.

Alison shivered as she remembered how wonderful it had been to lie in Brady's arms all night long. But her father had discovered them at dawn and insisted on annulling the hasty marriage. He and Brady had had a major fight, but Alison had finally given in to her father's demand, although the incident had caused a rift between them for months. Brady had kissed her and promised her the paper didn't make a difference, that he would forever be married to her in his heart.

And he had been for the first three years he was in the service. Then he'd suddenly stopped writing. She'd tried to contact him, to find out what was wrong, had sent him dozens of letters a week, but he never replied. Finally, when he started sending her letters back unopened, Alison had given up and forced herself to accept the fact that Brady's love for her had died, that he'd probably found someone else.

She swallowed back emotions as she ran a finger over the outline of his bad-boy face. Dammit. Why did just the sight of his chiseled features, that thick, jet-black hair, his wide jaw, that nose that had been broken in a teenage fight—why did that face still cause her insides to purr with desire?

And why had Grammy Rose included the photo in Alison's hope chest, especially now, when another man had proposed to her?

Maybe the photo was to remind her of her spontaneous marriage, the veil a hint to marry in a traditional ceremony this time. Expecting a note of explanation inside the envelope, she hurriedly opened it, but she sucked in a sharp breath when she saw the contents—her marriage certificate and the annulment papers that had ended her marriage to Brady.

Only Wiley and Grammy knew about the short marriage; she'd never even told her sisters. They'd both been away at college, each with their own problems. Did Grammy think Alison needed the papers to get a license to marry Thomas?

She quickly scanned the pages, the blank lines for their signatures, the blank line for the notary... The *blank* lines? Dear heavens, the papers had never been signed. She skimmed the note from her grandmother. "Honey, I'm so sorry. Wiley asked me to file these, but I suppose I forgot." Alison's heart pounded as she realized the implications.

She was still married to Brady Broussard.

Chapter Two

Alison's head was still reeling the next morning as she headed to the Fourth of July parade. She wiped perspiration from her forehead, half hoping it would rain to alleviate the drought they'd been having. But of course, rain would ruin the day's festivities.

Making matters worse, yesterday Vivica had shown up to talk about her wedding arrangements, and had informed her Brady was on his way home. Alison hadn't had time to recover from seeing the annulment papers; now she'd have to face Brady and tell him they were still married.

He hadn't been home since he'd left for the Air Force.

Could he possibly be returning to see her?

No, he was obviously coming for Vivica's wedding. He hadn't contacted Alison in almost a year—ten months and eleven days, to be exact. Not that she'd counted.

Hurt squeezed at her chest again, followed by confusion. All these years apart, she and Brady had both thought their marriage had ended, that they were free to go on and find someone else. Had Brady done that?

The memory of his kiss on her lips, his promise to love her forever brought a fresh wave of pain. But he hadn't loved her forever. He'd cut her out of his life without an explanation. And she'd given him her heart and soul. And her innocence.

In fact, she hadn't been able to give herself to anyone else since. Could it be because she'd still felt married to Brady? Heck, technically she *was* still married to him.

Maybe when she saw him today, she would realize they'd both changed and she'd finally be able to exorcise him from her mind. She squared her shoulders, waved to a few of the people she knew as she searched the growing crowd for her sisters, and tried to brace herself just in case she and Brady crossed paths during the day. Of course, with a kazillion people in town for the festivities, that would be unlikely.

Besides, she had to decide what to do about Thomas.

Planning other people's weddings and seeing her sisters so happily married had definitely given her the bug for a family of her own. Thomas wanted kids, a house in the suburbs, the whole nine yards. His proposal bounced around in her mind, along with all his positive characteristics, just as she rounded the corner and bumped into him.

"Hey, Alison." A grin lit his green eyes. *Kind* eyes. Yes, Thomas was a kindhearted, considerate, ambitious, stable man who would make a wonderful husband. He slid his fingers through hers and squeezed her hand, then whispered in her ear, "I was hoping we could talk after the parade."

Alison's stomach quivered. Was Thomas expecting an answer today?

BRADY HAD BARELY GOTTEN off the plane when his sister and mother launched themselves into his arms. Then they shoved him in the car to go to the Fourth of July celebration, and he felt himself fast losing control of his life.

"Mom, I told you I didn't want to go to the parade."

She smiled sweetly, cranked up her Thunderbird and tore down the highway, ignoring his protests as she launched into complaints about the recent drought. "We haven't been able to water the lawn for weeks. They've got us on one of those rotating schedules."

"Yeah, the water police come around daily to check," his sister said with a giggle.

Brady tried to smile, thinking the dying grass and shrubs resembled the way he felt inside.

"Honey, we're so proud you're here," his mother chirped. "You know one reason we have the parade is to honor the veterans, especially men who've given their lives for us." She gestured toward his leg. "And all those who've been injured."

"In case you haven't noticed, Mom, we haven't been at war lately. And I wasn't hurt in battle." Quite the opposite, he thought, as renewed guilt gripped his stomach.

"Nevertheless, your father served our country.

He'd want you to be there in his place to honor the veterans just as he always did.''

Brady's throat closed. That he couldn't argue with. He did respect veterans and all other soldiers, but he could never take his father's place. God knows he'd tried. He'd failed miserably, though.

''Relax, it'll be fun,'' Vivica whispered. She leaned over the edge of his seat and patted his leg. ''All your old friends will be there. Johnny and Bobby Raye and, oh, Alison will probably be there, too. I think her daddy, Wiley, is the grand marshal of the parade. You know he was in the navy himself when he was young.''

Brady glared at Vivica, but an image of Wacky Wiley Hartwell as grand marshal flashed in his mind, and he couldn't contain a smile. Wiley had a reputation for cheesy, funny advertising stunts and was somewhat the clown of Sugar Hill. But the last time Brady had seen the man in person, Wiley hadn't been happy. He'd just discovered he had a son-in-law, had reared up like a mother bear protecting its baby cub, and ordered Alison to get an annulment.

''Is he still as flamboyant as ever?'' Brady asked.

''Is he ever!'' Vivica said. ''I heard he wore a ruffled shirt to Hannah's and Mimi's weddings.''

''Last Thanksgiving he had live turkeys in one of his used-car ads,'' his mother added with a chuckle. ''I thought they were going to gobble up the old coot.''

''Alison said he's wearing his Uncle Sam top hat and coat for the parade,'' Vivica added.

Brady tried not to react to the sound of Alison's

name as he rubbed at his leg. The familiar scenery along the north Georgia highway rolled past, the parched grass and dry ground evidence of the drought across the southeast.

"Is your leg bothering you much?" his mother asked, her voice riddled with concern.

He ground his teeth, not wanting to worry her. "It's fine, Mom."

Vivica must have sensed his discomfort. "It'll be like new with some therapy. Just wait till I work my magic hands on him, Mom."

"I can't wait," Brady mumbled. "I've heard you're worse than a drill sergeant."

"Whatever cures ya," Vivica said with a wink.

He gave her a grateful half smile, but she ruined his mood. "By the way, did I tell you Alison's dating—"

"About a dozen times already." He sighed and lay his head back, pretending disinterest. "I think I'll rest until we get there. It was a long flight." And another long, sleepless night.

Vivica lapsed into silence and he silently cursed himself for being short with her. But he didn't want pity, not for his injuries, not for his personal life. He'd sit through the parade, then hightail it back to his mother's.

An hour later, they pulled into town, and he grimaced. The town square had been roped off, re-routing traffic in a wide loop to avoid food vendors, crafters and various other booths. The town bustled with activity, with locals eating hot dogs, preparing for an old-fashioned cakewalk, watering the ponies for the kids. His mother parked and they got out of the car—right in front of some town dignitaries. To his surprise, the mayor greeted him personally.

"Let me shake the hand of one of our own heroes." Mayor Stone pumped his hand, his ruddy face already flushed from the activities, a glob of unabsorbed sunscreen puddling on his bald head.

Brady's tongue completely tied itself into a knot with denials, but the mayor gave him no time for a reply. He immediately helped him onto a huge float draped in red-white-and-blue crepe paper resembling the flag. Brady felt like a fake among the other veterans as they rode down Main Street, waving at the kids and throwing candy. Children shouted while music blared from the high school band. The cheerleaders marched and chanted the familiar high school cheers. Shriners zipped by in go-carts, doing wheelies to entertain the crowd. Clowns passed out balloons to the children, followed by several antique cars carrying local beauty contestants—Little Miss Sugar Hill, Miss Teenage Sugar Hill, Little Mr. Sugar Hill. Unfortunately, the veterans float followed the line dancers and horses—a bad choice, Brady realized, when two of the huge mares decided to relieve themselves in front of them.

Oblivious to the problem, Wacky Wiley belted out a speech about all the servicemen and women and how they were heroes for their country, naming each person on the float. The high school band burst into a slightly off-key version of "The Star Spangled Banner" in the background.

Brady grimaced when Wiley called his name, his mind shouting that he wasn't a hero, that he didn't deserve to be up here with these other men. But

Wiley continued, and Brady scanned the crowd for familiar faces. He spotted a few of his high school teachers, the football coach he used to think hung the moon, some high school football buddies. Hannah Hartwell was standing beside a big, dark-headed guy, her arm tucked in his. Must be the cop Vivica said she'd married. A pregnant Mimi Hartwell stood beside them next to a sandy-haired man.

Finally he spotted *her*—Alison.

Beautiful sweet Alison wedged in the crowd, yet sticking out from all the others like a diamond in a case full of cut glass. She was even more beautiful than he remembered. She'd trimmed her waist-length black hair to her shoulders, but the shorter length made her look even more lively than ever. Though she was still tall and slender, her curves appeared more pronounced, more womanly and enticing, especially in that slinky, pale blue sundress. For a brief moment, he allowed himself to savor the sight of her, to remember what it felt like to hold her, to kiss those tender lips, to touch those luscious breasts with his hands, to have made her his wife....

The float jerked, then inched on, turning the corner by the hardware store, and Brady's gaze landed on the man beside her. Medium build, dull brown hair, scrawny, probably couldn't bench-press his own weight. He had to be Emerson, the doctor she was dating. Even if Vivica hadn't warned him, Brady would have known by the way the man was looking at her, drooling like a Saint Bernard.

Damn. He thought he'd been prepared to see her with another man, but he wasn't. The anguish nearly made his good leg buckle.

Just as he grabbed the edge of the float for support, Alison looked up from the crowd. Their gazes collided, locked. Time slipped away…. The driver whipped the float around the corner and Brady leaned forward, craning his head so he could still see her. But the float jerked again and he toppled off headfirst, right into the horse's behind in front of him.

ALISON'S FINGERS SLID from Thomas's hand and fluttered to her chest. Brady Broussard was riding on the float. Dear heavens, she hadn't been prepared for the sight of him in that Air Force uniform.

Or the fact that he simply stared right through her as if she wasn't there.

Hurt clogged her throat, pushing tears to her eyes, but she blinked them away, furious at herself for still caring. And for still being mesmerized by the man.

And he was definitely a man now—bigger, more muscular, tougher looking. She'd known all that thick black hair would be cut military style, but she hadn't imagined it showcasing the strong angles and planes of his face so well. The man was twice as sexy as he'd been in high school and college.

But more distant than ever.

Thomas yanked on her hand and a wave of dizziness assaulted her. She couldn't marry Thomas when she already had a husband, especially when they still had things unresolved between them. Like their annulment.

"You want a soda or one of those snow cones, Ali?" Thomas asked.

Dear heavens, he was always so considerate, and

here she was—a *married* woman dating him, and she hadn't even told him.

She shook her head. "No, but we need to talk."

Horns blasted from the parade, the fire engine blared its siren, children screamed and the grand finale—a pig named Elmer that had placed first prize at the country fair, and its owner, the winner of the hog-calling contest—rolled past, emitting grunts and squeals that could wake the dead.

The crowd began to disperse, all heading toward the festivities. Mimi waved. "I'd better get to the coffee shop. We'll be bombarded all day."

Seth curved his arm protectively around Mimi and guided her through the crowd. "And I'm going along to make sure she doesn't overdo it."

"We'll check out the booths. I see some dolls to add to my collection," Hannah said.

"Uh, I think I have to help direct traffic," Jake teased.

Hannah laughed and yanked Jake's hand, leading him away. "No, you don't. You promised me the entire day."

Alison laughed and waved to several people she knew, but Thomas coaxed her the other way, ending up beneath the awning of Sugar Hill's Hotspot, the new coffee shop-bookstore Mimi and their cousin Rebecca co-owned.

Thomas folded Alison's hands in his and pressed them to his chest. She could feel his heart beating, could see the anticipation in his eyes. "You look great today, Ali."

She smiled, wishing she could sugarcoat what she

had to say. Thomas was just so darn nice. "I…we have to talk."

"I know. I hope you've been thinking about my proposal."

She inhaled a deep breath. "I have, Thomas, and you're a wonderful guy."

His smile slipped slightly. "Uh-oh, that sounds like the beginning of a brush-off."

She pulled her hands free and laid one hand against his cheek. She wanted to love him. She just needed time to talk to Brady, sort out this annulment, put the past behind her forever. "I need some more time, Thomas. It feels like we're rushing things."

He studied her for a long moment, his expression calm and understanding. "Okay, take all the time you need. I'll be here whenever you're ready."

He was too good to be true.

Alison pressed a kiss to his cheek. "Thank you, Thomas."

Before she could elaborate, Vivica bounced up behind her. "Ali! Hey, look who's here."

Alison spun around, her breath whooshing out when she saw Brady standing beside her.

BRADY'S JAW ACHED from forcing a smile on his face. He'd been congratulated by at least a dozen people when he'd gotten off the float. Thankfully, Vivica had rescued him and heralded him through the crowd. Now he knew why. She'd purposely dragged him right to Alison.

When he'd seen Alison kiss Emerson Brady had

clenched his jaw harder, bitten his tongue and almost cracked a tooth.

"Dr. Emerson, this is my brother, Brady," Vivica said, smoothing over the awkward moment by launching into a long diatribe about how she and Brady had known Alison in high school. Brady shook the man's hand, studying Alison out of the corner of his eye. He tried to read her reaction—hurt, anger, disappointment or a combination of them all?

She had a right to be hurt, he thought. He had broken promises, stopped writing, sent her letters back even after she'd pleaded with him to write and explain what had happened to change his feelings toward her.

She'd be even more disappointed if she knew the truth about him now.

"Brady, aren't you going to give your old friend a hug?" Vivica nudged him forward. "I swear you and Alison are acting like you've never met."

He forced himself to hold out a hand, his insides clenching when she placed her long slender fingers in his and squeezed. "It's good to see you again, Alison."

"Brady." Her dark expressive eyes flickered with emotions.

"How long are you in town for?" Emerson asked, seemingly unaware of the tension between them.

"About a month." Brady adjusted his hat, aware that Alison followed the movement. Aware she also saw the long jagged scar on his hand. There were others she couldn't see. Some he would never reveal to anyone. "Maybe longer."

Alison's jaw went slack.

"He came home for the wedding." Vivica tucked her hand through his arm. "I asked him to run interference between me and Mom with the wedding plans. If it was up to her, I'd have three thousand guests, a full string orchestra, and the ceremony would be televised."

Alison smiled slightly, obviously trying to recover from the shock of learning Brady planned to stay in town all month. "She reminds me a little of Dad."

Vivica and Emerson laughed, and Brady gritted his teeth again. Was the man always so damn friendly? It was downright irritating.

"Brady, guess what?" Vivica tugged on his arm. "Alison owns the bridal shop in town, Weddings to Remember. She's coordinating the wedding for me."

Brady's mouth fell open this time, but he quickly snapped it shut.

"Since you offered to pay for the wedding, you'll need to work with her about finalizing all the details."

Brady shot Vivica a murderous look. His sneaky, conniving sister had set him up.

A beeper chirped and Emerson checked his, then threw an arm around Alison. "I hate to leave the celebration, but duty calls." He grinned. "Babies like to pick their own schedule. Of course, it's usually during the middle of the night."

He pecked Alison on the cheek, making Brady's

blood boil with all his friendliness and attentiveness, then said goodbye and sauntered away.

"I have to run, too," Vivica said. "Got to go see if I can find that fiancé of mine so I can introduce the two of you, Brady."

She flitted away, leaving Alison and him alone.

Alison turned grave eyes to him and he fisted his hands by his sides. He wanted desperately to apologize for the way he'd treated her, to explain about the training exercises that had taken him away for months, the accident that had scarred him for life, his uncertain future, but that would mean explaining about his friend's death and his part in it.

And he could never tell her or his family about that.

Of course, she'd gotten over him anyway, or she wouldn't be seeing another man and considering marriage to him.

ALISON BIT DOWN ON her lower lip, furious with Vivica for deserting her. Although Vivica didn't know the entire story about the wedding and annulment, she did know Alison had written Brady daily. And that he'd broken her heart.

Why would she do this to her?

One of the ladies from church nudged her in passing, and Alison forced her thoughts back to Brady. He was standing ramrod straight, military style, his expression as hard and ungiving as the dry ground beneath her feet. So different from the friendly, easygoing way Thomas looked at her. And the hungry way Brady used to look at her.

The sooner she told him about their little problem the better.

"I...we need to go somewhere and talk."

His dark brow raised slightly. "Now?"

She could have sworn his voice quivered. "If you have time. It's..." She twisted her hands in her skirt. "It's important."

"Is there a problem already concerning Vivica's wedding?"

"No."

He studied her, his lips pressed into an unbending line. "Can't you say what you have to say here on the street?"

Alison glanced around at the crowd. Oh, no, she didn't think that would be a good idea. But she might as well ask for the annulment, because Brady certainly didn't look as if he'd come to rekindle their relationship. "Let's go to my shop. It's closed today, so we can speak in private."

Chapter Three

Brady winced, feeling awkward and absurdly large, as he stepped inside Alison's frilly bridal shop. The lacy white fabrics and pictures of bridal gowns, invitations and other paraphernalia reminded him of his own wedding to Alison—and the simplicity of their ceremony.

But the vows had still been very real to him.

His hand once again pressed over the inside pocket to make certain her letters were still there, although he knew they were safely tucked within. He checked a hundred times a day. It had become a habit.

She turned to study him, her gaze resting on his injured leg. "Vivica didn't tell me you'd been hurt."

He shrugged. "I'm OK. I wanted to be here for Vivi's wedding."

Alison's dark eyes searched his face. For a brief second, he allowed himself to imagine her touching him.

"So you're a bridal consultant now?"

Alison smiled and glanced around the shop. "Yeah, go figure."

"I always thought you'd wind up teaching swimming or maybe being a counselor."

So he remembered she'd been on the swim team and that she played referee between Mimi and Hannah. "Yeah, well, things change, don't they?"

He nodded. "Time does that to people."

She looked away, stared at a gold chest in the corner that resembled a treasure chest, then bit down on her lip again.

"Why did you want to talk to me in private?" he asked.

Her eyes hardened for a moment, as if he should know the reason. And he did; he just couldn't bring himself to apologize or explain why he had stopped writing.

"There's something I have to show you."

He watched hungrily as she glided across the room, the blue dress brushing her bare legs as she knelt and opened the chest. She drew out an envelope and stood, then gestured toward a seating area with a low-slung white sofa and a dark green wing chair. "I think you'd better sit down."

What the hell did she have in the envelope? "I'm fine standing." Besides, he'd need help getting up off that sofa, and he certainly didn't want her helping him or feeling sorry for him.

"Really, Brady. I think this might come as a shock."

He studied her for a long moment, then finally conceded and took the chair, knowing he'd be able to get out of it easier. It took him a minute to stretch out his leg, another to look up at her without revealing the pain the movement cost him.

She was watching him when he did, a lost, soulful look that reminded him of that night at the lake. The night she'd cried because he was saying goodbye.

"I think you'd better take a look at this."

She handed him the envelope, and he breathed in the scent of lilacs, the same fragrance she'd worn four years ago. God, this was torture.

"I want you to know I received those papers only yesterday."

He frowned and opened the envelope, his hand shaking when he pulled out the marriage certificate. Then he removed the next set of papers and studied the text, his hands tightening around the pages.

"It's the annulment papers," Alison said in a low voice. "My grandmother sent them to me in the mail with my hope chest."

So that's what the gold chest was. Didn't women have hope chests when they were planning on getting married? The realization hit him full force. Alison was planning to marry Emerson. "I see." His gaze rose to meet hers, his throat thick. "But there are some missing signatures, and the papers haven't been processed. What's going on?"

"Apparently Dad asked Grammy Rose to file them and she forgot."

It took a nanosecond for him to realize the implications. When he did, he jerked his gaze to her. "Then…we're…"

"That's right, Brady. Technically, we're still married."

AND WE HAVE BEEN *for the last four years.*

Alison let the unspoken words stretch between them. Shock settled on Brady's face, then his eyes mellowed. With memories of the night he'd proposed, the night their young love had propelled them into each other's arms, into consummating their love by the lake, then into marriage.

Brady suddenly stood. The papers fluttered to the floor as he slowly reached out and touched her hair. His familiar scent filled her nostrils, his hungry gaze trapped her with its heat, and she moved toward him, cupped his face with her hands and melted into his arms.

He lowered his head, his breath ragged as he captured her lips and settled his mouth on top of hers, then delved inside with his tongue to taste her passion. The years fell away, the pain, the lonely nights and days, until Alison found herself clinging to his arms.

But she'd promised herself she would never cling or beg or force him to come back to her if he didn't want her. And she hadn't intended for the papers to do that.

She pulled away, slowly at first, then realized she had to distance herself or she might shatter and forget those promises she'd made to herself. As easily as he'd forgotten the ones he'd made to her.

"Alison... I—"

"No, don't." She turned and wrapped her arms around her waist, a nervous laugh bubbling inside when she saw the wedding picture of her and Brady. She'd been in her prom dress, so young, so in love, so naive....

"Alison, I'm sorry."

The gruffly spoken words made tears burn her eyes.

"I wish I could explain what happened, but I...I'm afraid I can't."

"We've both grown up," Alison said, squaring her shoulders.

"And changed."

The nervous laughter escaped. "Right, we were only kids back then. Foolish and impulsive and full of dreams."

"And stars." He cleared his throat. "But life changes and goes on."

She turned to face him and saw the strains of fatigue and worry etched on his face. He had aged, she realized, and a hardness, an emptiness had settled into his eyes that hadn't been there before.

What had happened to put it there?

She wanted desperately to know, yet self-preservation kicked in and she decided she couldn't ask. Not with that wall of broken trust between them.

"I...I really didn't know about the papers until yesterday. I'll file them as soon as possible, if that's what you want."

His expression grew even harder, even colder, if that were possible, the tension between them palpable. "I think that would be best." Then he turned and walked out the door, shutting it behind him.

Alison watched him limp down the street, and wondered at his choice of words. He hadn't said it was what he wanted, he'd said he thought it would be best. Her fingers brushed across her lips, and the memory of the passion in his kiss rose to taunt her. Could it be possible? Could Brady still have feelings for her? Or was she overanalyzing what he'd said, trying to hold on to some sliver of hope for their future?

BRADY WAS TOO SHAKEN to deal with the crowd in Sugar Hill, much less his doting, but slightly over-bearing mother. He did find Vivica and meet her fiancé, Joe, an architect, who seemed like a decent enough guy and appeared to adore Vivica. But Brady couldn't focus; he was trying to absorb the news that he and Alison were officially still married.

"The fireworks display is supposed to be even bigger this year," Vivica said.

"I've never been to a small-town one," Joe admitted. "We usually go into Atlanta."

"Hey, Vivi," Brady said, "would you and Joe give Mom a ride home, and let me take the car?"

"Aren't you going to stay for the fireworks?" Vivica asked.

Brady jammed his hands in his pockets. "I'm tired. If you don't mind, I'd like to head home. It's been a long day."

"Of course." Vivica dug in her purse for her keys and handed them to him. "I keep forgetting it hasn't been long since the accident. You need to rest."

He grimaced and shook Joe's hand. "See you later."

Although he'd intended to go home, he found himself driving out to the lake, sitting by the edge, looking at the chapel across the water. As he threw rocks into the lake and watched them sink to the bottom, he contemplated the downward spiral his life had taken.

And he remembered the last time he and Alison had been here together. The night they'd made love.

He shouldn't have kissed her back at her shop, but the kiss had been so natural, so damn full of uninhibited passion that he'd forgotten the reason he'd returned to town. The reasons he'd broken things off with her.

He'd nearly forgotten he couldn't be with her again.

Although it was seven o'clock, the hot July sun was still beating down fiercely on his neck, and he swiped at the perspiration on his brow. A headache pulsed behind his eyes, due to the strain and the aftereffects of the head injury he'd suffered in the accident, so he lay back on the grassy hill and closed his eyes. Memories of his high school days, of football games and dances and Alison, floated in and out of his consciousness, and he finally drifted into a deep sleep. But in his sleep, he was suddenly thrust back into that last training maneuver, the simulated combat mission in the Arizona mountains, the horrible accident....

The sound of Josh's panicked voice rang in his ears. "Caught his jet wash!"

The third jet turned and flew left.

Brady gritted his teeth. Josh was the best pilot he knew. He could handle it. "Hang in there, Shooter."

"No, not good," Josh mumbled.

"The bogey's right on me," Brady called. "Got to drop altitude." He dropped and exhaled as the bogey zoomed ahead.

Josh cursed. "Damn. My engines are down!"

Brady glanced sideways and saw Josh's fighter jet fly into a spin.

Brady hung a right onto Josh's tail. "Pull it up, man, pull it up."

"Can't. Out of control." The radio crackled. "This is bad…can't get her back."

Brady saw the mountain coming at them. Josh's plane's belly skimmed a rocky peak, clipping one of the wings.

"Lost the other engine!" Josh shouted. "Mayday! Mayday!"

Brady had to do something, had to help his friend! But the bogey was coming back toward him. "Eject! Eject, Shooter! Hit the eject button."

Josh's voice rasped out, "Can't reach it."

"Dammit, man, eject now! And watch the canopy!"

"Eject button malfunctioning!"

Brady's hands tightened on his own controls as Josh tried to crash-land, the jet shimmying wildly in its nose dive toward the valley. Another mountain came at Brady and he barely pulled up in time. The bogey pulled up and circled back. Josh hit the trees, skimmed along atop them, then plunged into the mountain.

Brady grappled with his own aircraft. Seconds later, his heart pounding, he landed, barely missing a nearby military building on the edge of the mountain as he rammed into the forest. Even before the plane stopped completely, he was undoing his seat belt. The jet's nose hit a tree and the impact threw him forward, his head slamming the control panel.

Then he was fighting to get out, running across the terrain.

An explosion suddenly rent the air. The wing of Josh's jet blew off and shards of metal slammed against his leg, knocking him to the ground. Another explosion shook the rocks, causing them to collapse. His foot was trapped, caught beneath the rubble. He yanked, tore at the debris, dragged his limb free. Pain shot through him. His leg was twisted and mangled, but he dragged himself forward. He clawed at the burning wreckage, frantically trying to pry open the door.

Blood spurted from his arm; metal scalded his hands; pieces splintered, slammed into his head. He tried to crawl inside, but the wreckage was an inferno. Josh…God no!

Brady jerked awake, trembling and sweating, the horror of Josh's twisted body still vivid, his own screams ringing in his ears. Where was he? The lake? But he'd heard an explosion.

Fireworks.

The town had started their evening show with a burst of patriotic red and blue colors. He must have slept for over two hours, for night had fallen. A skyful of stars twinkled above the lake, and the moon shone like a beacon. Just the way it had the night he and Alison had made love here. So damn long ago.

Another lifetime.

The marriage, the annulment—the sheer reality of it all crashed on top of him, almost as painful as the explosion had been. Alison had fallen in love with the star football player, the adventurous guy who planned to be a fighter pilot, the man who'd intended on spending his life serving his country, a hero.

If he and Josh hadn't been trying to best each other in the flying maneuvers, Josh might have realized the bogey was on him before he got caught in the other plane's jet wash. Brady couldn't escape the guilt that he had survived and Josh hadn't.

He looked down at himself in disgust, stared at the ugly scar twisting around his hand, at his leg, which was scarred and ugly beneath his pants. He was a broken shell of a man. Alison deserved a whole man. How could he have done anything but ask her to file the papers?

"YOU'RE AWFULLY QUIET, sis. Something wrong?"

Alison glanced at Hannah and forced a smile. Other than the fact that she had just watched the fireworks with three very-much-in-love couples on top of a beautiful hill overlooking the meadow by the lake, and she was alone, she was fine. Jake, Seth and Joe had gone for lemonade, momentarily leaving her with her sisters and Vivica.

"Alison?"

"I'm just tired, I suppose."

Mimi leaned closer. "Where's Thomas?"

Good grief. She hadn't even thought about him. "He had another delivery. Seems like the Fourth is a big day for babies."

Mimi laughed and patted her stomach. "I'm glad I have a few more weeks."

"Did you get a chance to talk to Brady?" Vivica asked.

Alison tried not to let his name affect her. "Yes, for a few minutes."

"How's he doing, Vivi?" Hannah asked. "Jake and I saw him walking toward the Thunderbird. He looked as if he was limping."

"He had an accident." Vivica frowned. "I'm going to help him with physical therapy while he's home."

"Why didn't you tell us he'd been hurt?" Mimi asked.

Vivica shrugged. "He asked me not to say anything to anyone."

Alison struggled with her emotions. "What happened, Vivi?"

Vivica ran her fingers through her pixie hair. "I don't know exactly, some kind of crash during a training maneuver. He won't talk about it."

That sounded exactly like Brady, Alison thought. He'd keep everything to himself, all his troubles, his pain. He always had to be the tough guy.

She had to be tough, too. After her parents divorce, she'd heard her mother arguing with Wiley. "I can't stand married life. That baby's always clinging to me."

That baby had been her.

Alison had made up her mind then she would never cling to anyone, and she wouldn't cling to Brady now.

"So, what did you tell Thomas?" Vivica asked.

Alison jerked her head up, surprised at the change in subject. How pathetic—she was still starved for any word about Brady. "I told him I needed time to think about it.'' *And I need time to end my first marriage.*

She opened her mouth to confide in them, then realized she couldn't, not now. Vivi and her sisters would want to know details, but her feelings were too raw to discuss with even her closest friend and her sisters.

The men sauntered back, laughing and joking, each heading toward his loved one. Alison suddenly felt out of place. The crowd was breaking up, so she said good-night, then headed toward her car, remembering her conversation with Brady. She'd told him she'd file the annulment papers as soon as possible so she could move on with her life.

But who could she get to file them? She didn't want the whole town to find out about her hasty marriage, to gossip and pry. She could see the headlines ''Town bridal consultant divorces.'' She needed a lawyer, someone who would be discreet.

Her mother.

A ball of anxiety knotted her stomach. She'd promised herself she'd never ask Janelle Hartwell for anything. After all, for more than twenty years she'd been a non-existent parent. Alison had been three when Janelle had deserted them. So she barely even remembered her. She and Hannah and Mimi had always depended on their father, Wiley. He'd been wonderful, except for that one night—the night he'd forced Alison to have the annulment.

And now she was back in that boat again.

The very reason she was thinking about her mother, the lawyer. Dear heavens, she'd refused Janelle's offer of financial aid when she'd decided to open the bridal shop; she hated to go to her now. But Donald Matthews and her mother were the only two lawyers in town. Matthews's secretary Wanda had a mouth like a party line. Janelle was the only one Alison could swear to secrecy.

She glanced over her shoulder and saw Jake and Hannah, Mimi and Seth, and Vivica and Joe all walking hand in hand toward their cars, and felt more alone than ever. She didn't want to be alone forever. And Brady didn't want her—he'd made it clear when he'd stopped writing, and then again today. She had to accept his decision.

Knowing she shouldn't put off the inevitable, she dug through her purse for her cell phone, swallowed a big chunk of pride, punched in her mother's number, and left a message on her machine.

Chapter Four

"It's nice to have you home." Brady's mother placed a heaping plate of pancakes in the center of the table, along with a pitcher of maple syrup and a bowl of fresh strawberries, all the time complaining about how the heat had affected her garden. "We need a man around this house."

Brady's hand tightened around his coffee cup.

Vivica rolled her eyes. "We don't *need* a man, Mom. We've managed fine on our own." She winked at her brother. "But it is nice to have you here, Brady."

He smiled, grateful for her interference, and stabbed some of the hotcakes. "Do you need some yard work done or something, Mom?"

"Heavens no, the grass is dying from lack of rain." His mother scooted a plate of sausages toward him. "You eat up, now, son. You look a little thin to me."

"I'm fine, Mom." Brady ignored the way she stared at him in concern. "But I must admit, I have missed your cooking."

"Just don't overdo it and get fat or you won't be

able to fit into your uniform when you return to duty,'' Vivica said.

Brady's fork halted in midair. *When* he went back? He wasn't sure if he would, but he hadn't told anyone yet.

Mrs. Broussard stirred sugar into her coffee. ''I thought you might decide to stay here. Won't they give you some kind of early medical discharge?''

''Mom,'' Vivica chided. ''Don't start bugging Brady to retire from the Air Force.''

''I thought he might have changed his mind about taking over the print shop.''

The pancakes were beginning to clump in Brady's stomach like rocks. He and his mother had argued about this over and over in the last few months. It was one reason he hadn't come home sooner. Trouble was, he wasn't sure he would ever fly again—and for the first time in his life, he was actually considering her suggestion.

Vivica pushed away from the table. ''Gotta run now. I want to catch Alison before I have to go to work.''

Brady watched Vivica hurry out the door. What would Alison think if she knew he was considering staying?

''I'M SO GLAD YOU WANTED to meet for breakfast.'' Janelle Hartwell laid her hand over Alison's. ''I want us to get together more often.''

Alison struggled not to immediately pull her hand free. ''This isn't a social visit.''

Disappointment flitted across her mother's face. ''Oh, then what exactly is it?''

Alison took a sip of her water, silently asking for courage. Her mother was dressed to the nines today in a designer suit. The perfect outfit made her seem standoffish, contradicting the almost overeager look in her eyes. If Alison didn't know better, she'd have thought her mother really wanted to be a part of her life. "I need your help."

Janelle studied her silently for a moment, her ruby lips slowly moving into a smile. "Of course, honey. What can I do for you?"

She should have asked that years ago, when Alison needed her to take her shopping for her first bra, explain the facts of life, show up at her swim meets... But she bit back the words. Hannah and Wiley and Grammy Rose had been there for all those things. And Alison couldn't dwell in the past. Not with her mother or with Brady.

She placed the envelope on the table, sipping coffee while her mother studied the papers. Finally her mother sent her a questioning look. "You were married?"

Alison nodded. "Brady and I dated his last year in high school, then he went to college and we kept in touch." She hesitated, not wanting to share too many details. "After his father died, we grew closer, then Brady joined the Air Force. The night before he was supposed to leave, we got married."

"Young and impulsive, huh?"

Alison smiled. "Exactly. But Dad found out the next morning and insisted we have the marriage annulled."

Janelle nodded, crinkling her eyes in confusion. "But he never filed the papers?"

"He asked Grammy to file them, but she forgot."
Alison twisted the napkin in her lap. "She sent them
to me a couple of days ago."

"I see."

The waiter delivered their breakfast, an omelette
for Alison, wheat toast and fresh fruit for her
mother. Janelle took a bite of her sliced peaches before continuing. "So you want me to file them?"

"Yes. As soon as possible." Alison leaned closer.
"And I'd like to keep this between us. I don't want
the town to know. I never even told Hannah or Mimi
about the marriage."

Janelle arched a brow. "All right, but why the
hurry?"

Alison shrugged and pushed the omelette around
on her plate, wishing she'd stuck with dry cereal.
"It's been almost four years. I'd hardly call that a
hurry."

Her mother smiled, smearing butter on her toast.
"I guess you have a point. But there may be a problem."

Alison's stomach protested the eggs, so she
sipped her orange juice instead. "What kind of
problem?"

"There are certain restrictions on the parameters
for annulment. You were both legally of age. You
aren't cousins or related in any way."

Alison nodded.

"There was no coercion involved—I'm assuming
he didn't force you into marriage?"

"No, of course not."

"Neither one of you were already married at the
time?"

She shook her head.

"One last thing—did you consummate the marriage?"

Alison's breath caught. Even as a grown woman, she found it way too weird having this conversation with her mother.

Janelle waited, studying her with a knowing look.

"Yes, we consummated the marriage."

Janelle nodded. "Well, then unless one of you can claim mental impairment, you don't fit the parameters for an annulment."

"What?"

"That's the law, honey."

"Then…then what do we do?"

"You'll have to file for a divorce."

Divorce. That seemed like such an ugly word, so much more hurtful than *annulment.*

"And how long will a divorce take?"

"About thirty days." Janelle poured more coffee, her voice low. "That is, if neither of you contests it."

BRADY HAD PROMISED his mom he'd stop by the print shop and help out for a while, but he'd also promised Vivica he'd meet her at Alison's to discuss wedding plans.

And of course, he needed to find out about the ending of his own marriage.

Dreading the thought of seeing Alison almost as much as the thought of not seeing her, he strolled down Main Street, noting changes in the town he hadn't noticed the day before. In the aftermath of the big celebration, the small community seemed unusually quiet, a peaceful blend of nostalgic antique shops and more contemporary businesses popping up. A recreation center had opened on the corner, he wondered if Alison swam there daily. He passed a new law office with the name Janelle Hartwell on the door—could that be Alison's mother, or had Wiley remarried? Moving along, he noticed a sign for Wacky Wiley's Used-Car Fourth of July Sale, then the Hotspot, which Vivi said Mimi had opened next to Alison's bridal shop. Everywhere he looked there seemed to be Hartwells.

His parents' print shop was situated a few doors down from Alison's store, with a photography shop and a dress boutique in between. Brady entered the Weddings to Remember shop, bracing himself to see Alison.

She stood behind a long counter filled with a selection of bridal books, crystal champagne flutes and bridesmaid gifts. A long, white, lacy wedding dress covered in pearl beads hung behind her on a padded hanger. As he drank in the sight of her, his vision blurred and he imagined Alison wearing the dress to their wedding.

The bell tinkled, announcing his arrival and shaking him back to reality. "Alison."

She looked up. "Brady."

At one time, she would have launched herself into his arms. Now she seemed wary, distant. What had he expected? "I'm supposed to meet Vivi here."

She nodded, adjusted a stack of brochures and walked around the counter. "Can I get you some coffee?" She gestured toward a corner table draped in a rose tablecloth, complete with coffee, condiments and sweet rolls.

He pressed his hand to his stomach. "No, thanks. Mom stuffed me this morning."

Alison's mouth curved into a smile and his gut clenched. He'd forgotten how her eyes sparkled with flecks of gold when she smiled. "I bet she loves having you home."

"I'll probably gain twenty pounds in a week."

A small laugh escaped her and he couldn't help but smile. God, he missed the sound of her voice and laughter.

"So, you want to sit down? Vivi should be here soon, then we can discuss the plans. I've worked out a tentative schedule to make sure all the details fall into place."

The shop seemed amazingly intimate as he limped to the sitting area and situated himself in the green chair again.

As if she read his mind, Alison said, "The shop shouldn't be very busy today. Everyone's probably gone into Atlanta to the big malls for the holiday sales." She rattled on for several minutes, filling him in on her sisters' jobs and how Mimi had come to own the coffee dessert shop. "So Mimi and Seth ended up together. They were married in the gazebo on Pine Mountain at Grammy Rose's, just like Hannah."

He nodded and was just about to open his mouth to ask how he could help with his sister's wedding plans when she continued. "I had breakfast with my mother this morning."

That surprised him. "I didn't know she was back in town."

"She came back a couple of months ago. We were all surprised."

He remembered Alison mentioning her mother once, not in a good way, either. "So, how is it?"

"Awkward as all get out."

Honest, forthright Alison.

"But we're managing. She set up a law office downtown."

"Oh, yeah, I saw it on my way over."

Alison nodded, gathered some paperwork he assumed had to do with his sister's wedding, and sat down on the love seat. Today she was wearing a peach-colored shell and a floral skirt that hit her midknee, showcasing those dynamite long legs. He tried not to think about how they'd felt wrapped around him, or how they would feel again.

"Anyway, I asked my mother to handle the annulment."

Oh, right, so Alison could marry someone else. "I see. And she agreed?"

"Yes, but there's a problem."

She didn't want the annulment? His heart missed a beat as he waited.

"Technically we can't annul the marriage. There are parameters for that." She listed several reasons. "And since the marriage was consummated…" A slight blush swept across her features, making her appear young and vulnerable again, reminding him of that night when she'd lain naked in his arms. "Well, unless one of us pleads mental incompetence, we have to file for a divorce instead."

"I guess we could both plead mental incompetence. We were only kids."

"Yeah, impulsive, crazy in love…" She laughed, a nervous sound this time.

"Crazy teenage hormones. But I don't suppose the judge would buy that." He forced a laugh, too, but the laughter died quickly, fading into awkwardness.

"Anyway, my mother agreed to file the papers for us. She said a divorce takes about thirty days, unless someone contests it." She fiddled with her notepad. "I told her to keep everything confidential, that I didn't want the whole town to know. Since I'm a wedding planner, a divorce might not be good for business."

So her job was more important than his feelings. And she probably didn't want her new boyfriend to know she'd married him.

Brady nodded, glancing sideways at the fake wedding cake sitting on the table. They hadn't had a cake the night they'd married, but they'd stopped at the doughnut shop, bought crème-filled doughnuts and fed them to each other to celebrate their union. Everything had been so simple—they hadn't cared about details. They'd only cared about being together.

Now she wanted to erase that past without anyone ever knowing they'd shared it.

ALISON WONDERED IF BRADY was remembering their wedding, the simple but romantic ways they'd celebrated. Maybe she could put their relationship behind her if she understood more about where it had gone wrong. He looked so lost and faraway that she forgot her pride.

"Why did you stop writing, Brady?"

His head jerked back to hers, his breathing raspy. But he quickly looked away, studied his hands, his shoes, finally resting his hands on his knees. "I intended to keep my promises when I left. But..."

"You met someone else?"

"No." His gaze flew to hers, a hint of desperation there, as if it was important to him that she believe him. "I was sent on a training assignment and was out of touch most of last year."

"That's when the letters stopped."

He nodded. "I couldn't contact anyone, not even my family, to let them know where I was."

"What about when you returned?"

"I intended to write you then, but we did some combat maneuvers in Arizona, and I had the accident."

"You were in the hospital?"

"About three months."

Alison's hand flew to her chest. "That serious? Vivi didn't tell any of us."

He nodded again, his eyes dark as he stretched his fingers in front of him and studied his hands. "I asked her not to say anything."

"Why not? You knew we'd be worried."

"Look, Alison, I'm sorry."

"Was anyone else hurt?"

Brady hesitated. "My best friend, Josh, was killed."

Alison's heart broke for him. "Oh, Brady, I'm so sorry."

"It's over now, but things change, Alison. People change." He flexed his hands, then balled them into fists. "When I was recovering, I realized I'd been away too long, that it was time for both of us to move on."

She frowned in confusion. "Because you lost your friend?"

His voice took on a hard edge. "Because you have your life here, and I have another life. Why keep writing, hanging on to silly teenage dreams? Like you said, we were impulsive kids. We're not anymore."

His words sounded so harsh, so final. Alison tried to absorb what he was saying and the things he wasn't saying. She had a feeling the parts he'd left out were as important as the things he'd openly revealed.

"When do you have to report back for duty?"

"In a month, but my enlistment time's almost up." He shifted, avoiding eye contact. "Mom's pressuring me to come home and run the print shop, and with Dad gone and Vivi moving to Atlanta, I'm…I'm considering it."

"What?" Alison couldn't have been more shocked if he'd said he wanted to open a bridal shop. "But, Brady, you hated working there in high school, even for the summer. You never wanted to do anything but fly."

"Like I said, Alison, things change. And so do people."

Alison stared at him in confusion. Some things did change, but Brady giving up flying? He couldn't have changed that much. Or could he?

Chapter Five

The bell on the door tinkled, interrupting them, and Vivica walked in, followed by Brady's mother. Brady breathed a sigh of relief, grateful for the change in subject.

"Hey, Brady, Ali, I'm sorry we're running late, but we got tied up looking for shoes at the mall."

Brady stood. "That's okay. Where's Joe?"

"He had to go back to Atlanta. He's trying to finish designs on a big shopping complex so he can take time off for the honeymoon," Vivica explained. "He gave me free rein, told me to do whatever I wanted for the wedding."

"We do need to do a fitting for your dress," Alison said. "The alterations may take time."

"Okay." Vivica plopped down onto the sofa. "But give me a few minutes. I'm worn-out."

Alison explained the checklist she used to make certain all the arrangements would be completed on time—the photographer, caterer, florist, reservations for the chapel, the wedding cake, invitations, bridesmaids' dresses, music.

"You're a dream," Vivica said, giving her a hug.

"I don't know how I'd get through this without you."

"It seems like you have everything under control," Brady commented. "You've turned into quite the businesswoman."

Alison smiled, obviously picking up on the admiration in his voice. "Thanks. Dad'll be glad to know college was worth something."

"Have you started plans of your own with Thomas?" Vivica asked.

Brady tensed, waiting for Alison's reply. Was she planning a big splashy wedding to Emerson?

Alison blushed. "Did Joe tell you about Thomas?"

"Of course." Vivica turned to Brady. "Joe and Thomas were college buddies. Thomas actually introduced me to Joe."

She turned back to Alison, and Brady ground his teeth. *So the four of them were chummy, huh? How nice.*

"He shouldn't have said anything," Alison stated in a low voice.

Vivica grinned, oblivious to their discomfort. "Even if he hadn't, Ali, this is Sugar Hill. Proposals and pregnancies are the stuff that keeps the gossip vine alive."

"You're pregnant?" Brady asked in a shocked voice.

"No!" Alison screeched. "And I haven't given Thomas an answer yet, Vivi."

Mrs. Broussard cleared her throat. "Vivica, honey, if you don't need me, I'm going to grab Brady and take him to the print shop."

Brady's chest tightened. Had he made a mistake by agreeing to help his mother temporarily? She was already dropping hints and pressuring him to stay permanently.

"Vivi, go on into the fitting room and start changing," Alison suggested. "I'll help you in a minute."

Brady's mother grabbed his arm.

"Mrs. Broussard, I need to discuss some things with Brady before you go. Maybe you can look over the invitation list and see if there are any names we need to add. We should get those printed and in the mail right away."

"Oh, certainly, dear."

Brady stiffened, not wanting to resume their earlier conversation about the accident. In fact, he didn't want to meet with Alison to plan his sister's wedding at all. Seeing her and not being with her was almost as painful as his throbbing leg. "We could get someone else to take care of the wedding arrangements if this is too uncomfortable."

"Don't be silly, Brady." Alison frowned. "Vivi's my best friend. I want to help plan her wedding."

He grimaced inwardly, angry that his hands itched to reach out and touch her. "All right, then."

She pointed to her desk calendar, a pastel-pink book with an inspirational verse about romance at the top of each page. "My mother wanted us to meet her for lunch tomorrow to discuss the divorce. How about noon?"

He adopted his best military expansion. She obviously wanted a quick divorce so she could marry Emerson. "Sure. We should get this over with as quickly and painlessly as possible."

She simply nodded.

Then he turned and walked toward the door, maintaining his rigid posture and gritting his teeth every step of the way.

ALISON FOLDED the underarm seam of Vivica's wedding gown and pinned it, then proceeded to tuck in the waist. "Brady seems different. Does he ever talk about the accident?"

Vivica shook her head, sucking in her tummy. "No, I wish he would. Frankly, I'm worried about him."

"I know. He said he's considering staying here and taking over your father's business."

"He what?" Vivica gasped, unintentionally letting out the breath she'd been holding. The fabric slipped and Alison stabbed her finger with the pin.

"Ouch."

"Oh, sorry."

"No big deal. Maybe it's too tight. We don't want you passing out halfway down the aisle."

Vivica laughed. "No, it's fine. I'm losing five pounds before the ceremony."

"You don't need to lose weight," Alison said with a laugh. "Joe seems perfectly happy with you the way you are."

"I know he's wonderful." Vivica relaxed. "But Brady's a mess. He can't stay here and run that print shop. He'll be miserable."

Alison tucked in the bodice, forming a small dart to make the bustline fit properly. "I know. All he ever wanted to do was fly. He used to go on and on about it in high school. He even wrote me and told me about how excited he was when he saw his first fighter jet.''

''I think he blames himself for the crash, but I'm not sure why.'' Vivi caught Alison's hand and forced her to meet her gaze. ''I was hoping you could get him to talk. You know—open up. You two were always so close, Ali.''

''But he's different now, Vivi. Distant, closed off.''

''Like he was ever a big talker?''

Alison chuckled. Vivica was right. She knew how stubborn Brady could be. Maybe this month-long wait would be good for both of them. If she got to know him again, she might realize they weren't compatible anymore and she could finally get over him.

BRADY STUDIED THE LAYOUT of the print shop and the orders his mother had taken for the day, easily fitting back into the routine of tasks he'd handled as a teenager when he'd helped his father during the summers. Stacks of papers, poster board, an ad layout for the hospital, the copy machines: everything came back to him as if he'd never left the place.

And so did the monotony.

Why had his father given up the Air Force to open this business? And how had he worked here for ten years without losing his mind?

Lack of stress.

Memories of his crash descended upon Brady, and he suddenly realized lack of stress was the reason he was considering staying here and taking over for his mother. If he didn't have to face flying every day, he might get over his guilt. Guilt that he'd left his mother to run the shop alone after his father had died, while he'd pursued his own dreams. Guilt over his friend's death. Guilt over not taking leave time when he'd had the chance.

His mother greeted a customer who wanted advertisements printed for the hospital benefit, and Brady busied himself with the smaller jobs, deciding to take the bookkeeping home and review it tonight when he couldn't sleep.

"Brady, hon, would you run off your sister's wedding invitations? I'm swamped with this hospital benefit."

"Sure, Mom." He gathered the information and began typing it in, grateful his mother had kept up with technology and invested in a good computer system. But while he automatically entered the date and time and place of the wedding, his thoughts turned to Alison and their wedding.

She'd been like a vision standing in the small moonlit chapel wearing her prom dress, a pale blue, silky, off-the-shoulder gown with a thigh-high slit. But it had been the love in her eyes that had totally hypnotized him.

When he'd married her, he'd thought it would be forever, just as he'd thought he would be in the Air Force forever. He'd imagined going overseas for a while, then maybe getting stationed in the States. Finally, after the kids came, he'd settle down and teach other recruits to fly. Maybe teach his own son to fly one day.

He stretched out his hands and stared at the scarred knuckles, trying to imagine them holding on to the controls again. But his pulse raced, sweat broke out on his brow and his hands began to tremble uncontrollably.

He couldn't do it, couldn't even think about climbing in the cockpit of a plane, much less getting behind the controls and actually flying. He closed his hands into fists, squeezing his eyes shut to banish the images of the explosion. But he could still see the fire licking at the cockpit, shooting from Josh's clothes, blazing its trail of horror.

No, he'd lost more than his friend in the crash; Brady had lost his will to fly. He had watched all his dreams go up in smoke right along with Josh.

"ALISON, THIS IS THOMAS. Can I come over?"

Alison adjusted the phone to her ear as she stared at the hope chest. She'd brought it home and placed it in her bedroom, and had forced herself not to look at the contents again, but she knew what lay inside. The photo of her and Brady on their wedding day. "Not tonight, Thomas, I'm really tired." *And confused and worried about Brady, the man I'm still married to.*

"Is everything all right? You sound kind of strange."

"I'm fine. I just need some…space. Please try to understand."

He hesitated, his usual cheery voice resonating with hurt when he spoke again. "All right. I didn't mean to bother you."

"You didn't, it's just…I have a lot to think about right now." Alison closed her eyes and sighed, feeling guilty for hurting him. But she had to be fair to him and to herself, and leading him on certainly wouldn't be fair.

"Will you call me when you're ready to talk?"

"Yes, Thomas, and…thanks for being so understanding. You really are wonderful."

"So are you, Ali. I'm looking forward to seeing you again."

She hung up, unable to shake the feeling of impending doom she'd had all day. While she'd worked on the arrangements for Vivica's wedding, she'd had visions of making wedding plans for herself.

Only Thomas's face hadn't appeared in her visions, Brady's had.

What if she was making a mistake? Letting Thomas go when the only thing left between her and Brady were memories? Was she hoping they might rekindle their love when the embers had died out and been buried in the dust years ago?

Feeling agitated, she went to her wicker desk and pulled out the box of letters Brady had written her. She'd saved every one from college and from his days in flight training. Lying back on her duvet, she turned on the Tiffany lamp her grandmother had given her for her sixteenth birthday, removed the first letter from the rubber band and opened it.

Dear Alison,
It's midnight here and every part of my body hurts, but I couldn't sleep without writing you about the first day. The training was ten times rougher than football practice. We got up before dawn, worked out like crazy, then ran ten

miles with our packs on, all before breakfast. The cots are hard, the lieutenant is a first-class psycho (he made the guy in the bunk next to me do a hundred push-ups just because his damn sheets weren't tucked in right), and the food stinks, but I saw one of the planes today and my heart just about exploded in my chest. I keep telling myself it'll all be worth it. One day I'll be able to fly a fighter jet by myself. Maybe I can borrow a Cessna at the airport in town when I come home and take you for a ride above the lake. We can stop and make love on the shore again, just like on our wedding night.

I hope your dad gets over being pissed off at me and realizes that although I'm in the Air Force, I'm not ever completely going away. Flying has always been in my soul, baby, but you're in my blood now, too. It doesn't matter if we've got papers or not, you'll always be my girl. Have sweet dreams thinking about me tonight 'cause you know I'll be dreaming about you.

I've got your picture here under my pillow. I wish I had your body here, too, so I could run my hands all over you and make you moan and say my name when I give you pleasure.

Love,
Brady

Alison folded the letter and tucked it back inside the envelope, her heart clenching. Flying had always been in his soul, so how could he possibly give it up? And if she'd truly been in his blood, how could he come back and act as if he didn't care for her anymore?

BRADY FINISHED LOOKING over the bookkeeping, a headache pounding through his brain. His mother was right: the books were a mess. She needed to hire someone to take over the finances right away. Maybe he'd help her find an affordable accountant before he… Before he what? Left town again?

Cursing beneath his breath, Brady poured himself a Scotch and limped to his bedroom, stripped down to his boxers and opened up the balcony doors to let in the fresh night air. Crickets chirped in the woods, a dog howled somewhere in the distance and a breeze stirred the trees, bringing the scent of his mother's roses. Though ancient trees flanked the backyard of his mother's house, offering privacy, he looked across the street, over the row of houses to the corner where Alison lived. Vivi had pointed out her apartment when they'd driven into town. It seemed odd that she'd chosen a place so close to his mother's house. From his two-story balcony, he could actually see a faint light burning from one of her windows. What was she doing? Was she awake? Getting ready for bed?

Did she have company?

Was Emerson touching her, kissing her? Making love to her?

Brady's hand tightened around the glass as he took a hefty swig, trying to extricate the images from his mind.

Tomorrow he and Alison would meet with her

mother to discuss the divorce. Soon Emerson would have free rein, and Brady would have nothing. No legal right to Alison. No right to her at all.

It had to be that way.

He glanced down at his scarred leg, the jagged, puckered skin below his boxers, pink and ugly in the moonlight. Tossing down the rest of the Scotch, he stepped back inside and grabbed his duffel. Unable to help himself, he pulled out the stack of letters Alison had written him over the years. He'd kept them bound with a rubber band and stuffed inside his bag wherever he went.

He thumbed through the stack, recognized the familiar lilac stationery she'd used to write the first letter, then stepped back onto the balcony and read it.

Dear Brady,

I can't believe you've been gone only hours. I'm already missing you so much I hurt, and I'm so mad at my dad I haven't spoken to him all night. I wish Hannah and Mimi were here to help me talk some sense into him, to make him realize that I'm not a kid anymore. I'm a grown woman now, *your* woman, Brady. I love you with all my heart, and I'll never forget how it felt to have you call me your wife, how it felt to lie naked in your arms and have you make love to me.

I have to admit I was a little scared about being intimate with you at first. You've always been so big and strong, and I love that about you, but you were so tender that night. I thought making love would be good, but I'd never imagined it would be so wonderful. I want you again, Brady. I wish you were here right now, and I could peel off this nightgown and feel your lips kissing mine, your hands on my breasts, your big strong body moving above me.

When you go to bed tonight, close your eyes and pretend you see me dancing naked in the moonlight. And when you look up into the sky and see the stars twinkling, you'll know I'm smiling down at you, whispering your name, begging you to come back to me.

I love you, forever & ever & always,
Alison

Brady clenched the letter in his fist. A friend of his had known about the letters. He'd brought them to Brady in the hospital. Brady had read them so many times he could recite the contents in his sleep.

But when he'd awakened in the hospital and remembered the horror of what had happened, when he'd seen the scars on his body, he'd also known his relationship with Alison would never be the same. She deserved someone better, a whole man.

Once the divorce was final, he'd have to get rid of the letters. And he'd have to forget he had ever had a woman like Alison Hartwell. And that for one glorious night she'd lain in his arms as his wife, Alison Broussard.

Chapter Six

"Come on, Brady, you're doing great. Just a few more reps and you can get in the whirlpool."

"You're enjoying torturing me, aren't you?" Brady gritted his teeth, shot Vivica a murderous look and tried to bend his leg as she'd instructed.

Vivica smiled sweetly. "Payback for that time you held me upside down over the toilet and tried to flush my ponytail."

Brady almost laughed. He had been a pretty aggravating brother at times. "It just made you tough."

Vivica laughed. "Right. I was scared to death of you for the first five years of my life. I had nightmares of you dropping me over the stair rail on my head."

"Yeah, but you were damn lucky I was around when all the boys started chasing you." Brady finished the set of exercises with a grunt.

"Uh-huh, I surely didn't want boys chasing me. Now let's try something else." Vivica placed his foot on her thigh, braced herself and forced him to push as hard as he could. Sweat trickled down his face, the agony in his leg compounded by the after-effects of a sleepless night.

"Thanks for being nice to Joe. That means a lot."

"He seems like a stand-up kind of guy." Brady's leg jerked, his muscles cramping, and Vivica helped him stretch it out, massaging the knotted muscle. "Anyway, I pretty much told him he'd be dead meat if he hurt you."

Vivica rolled her eyes. "You know we're moving to Atlanta after we're married?"

"Yeah."

"I hope Mom's going to be okay alone."

She may not be alone. "She wants you to be happy, Vivi."

"I know. She wants the same for you, bro. Even if she does hint that you should take over the print shop, she wouldn't want you to do it and be miserable."

He didn't comment, but then he didn't think his sister expected him to.

She held out her hand. "Come on, let's get you in the whirlpool. You deserve a little R and R."

Brady stiffened, shaking off her help as he grabbed the handrail and hauled himself to a standing position. "I don't deserve to be coddled, Vivi."

His sister hesitated, studying him. "Don't you think you're being a little hard on yourself? You had an accident, Brady, you didn't go out and intentionally—"

"Drop it, sis." Brady turned and walked away.

Vivica called after him, "And you should talk to the doctor about sleeping pills. I can tell by the dark circles under your eyes you're not resting."

Brady ignored her comment as he strode toward the whirlpool. He was determined to get the physical therapy session over with as soon as possible. After all, he didn't want to keep Alison and her mother waiting. They had a divorce to discuss.

ALISON STOOD in the entryway of the Red Robin Café, her stomach fluttering with nerves as she searched the room for her mother and Brady.

"Alison, hey, I didn't know you were going to be here."

She spun around, nearly whacking Thomas with her shoulder bag. "Oh, Thomas, I'm so sorry."

He laughed and rubbed at his elbow. "It's all right. I didn't mean to startle you."

"You didn't."

He raised a brow.

"Well, I guess you did. My mind must be a million miles away."

"Sorting through things."

"Yes." Like his proposal—and her relationship with the man she hadn't known she was still married to.

She spotted Brady lumber in, his face tight as he strode toward her. Either he was in a great deal of pain or he was angry about something. The room suddenly grew hot, almost as stifling as the dry heat outside.

How awkward. Her boyfriend with her husband—soon to be ex-husband.

"Alison, sorry I'm late," Brady said when he approached. "Vivica tried to kill me with therapy sessions."

So he was in pain. She ached to reach out and comfort him. But the fierce scowl he sent Thomas shocked her into silence. Then Brady's gaze traveled to her, and something dark and dangerous and sensual lurked in the hidden depths of his dark brown eyes. Something carnal and almost possessive.

A nervous laugh escaped her. "Oh, you're not late. Thomas and I were just chatting."

Thomas gave Brady the once-over as well. "Broussard, good to see you again."

Brady pumped his hand.

"Thomas is the new OB-GYN who works with Hannah," Alison explained.

Brady's jaw tightened considerably, and he moved his hand to her waist. "I know, Eberson and I met at the parade."

"Oh, I forgot." Alison said.

"It's Emerson," Thomas corrected.

"Right." Brady turned to Alison. "Are you ready for lunch?"

"We're meeting to talk about Vivi's wedding plans," Alison added when confusion reddened Thomas's face.

"Maybe we can catch a game of golf sometime," Thomas suggested.

"I don't play golf," Brady replied curtly.

"My mother's joining us for lunch," Alison said, instantly wondering why'd she offered that information.

"Your mother?" Thomas looked even more confused.

Alison bit down on her lip, but Thomas's pager beeped, saving the awkward moment.

"Another baby on its way," Thomas said with a grin. "Have a nice lunch, you guys. If you change your mind about the golf, just let me know."

Brady's dark gaze raked over Alison as Thomas left, and she shifted restlessly. Had he been jealous of Thomas?

BRADY JERKED HIS GAZE away from Alison, mentally calling himself a dozen unspeakable names for acting like such a fool. He had no claims on her.

Yes, you do. She's still your wife, a little voice inside his head whispered. *And in your heart, she always will be.*

No, he had to get over her. He had to end the marriage and forget her.

"Where's your mother?" he asked, a little more gruffly than he'd intended.

Alison searched the room, finally turning to look out the window, a nervous smile settling on her face when a tall, sleek, middle-aged blonde waved through the tinted glass.

Seconds later, Mrs. Hartwell appeared, smoothing down a strand of hair the wind had blown from her topknot. He'd wondered if she would resemble Alison, but except for her height, she didn't; she favored Hannah. As they were seated, the tension between the two women was palpable. "Janelle, this is Brady Broussard." Alison gestured to Brady. "Janelle Hartwell."

He shook her hand.

"It's nice to meet you, Brady. Call me Janelle." Mrs. Hartwell turned a charming smile toward him, and he realized she was sizing him up to see what kind of man her daughter had married four years ago. Of course, he'd always wondered what kind of woman could leave her children. But he didn't intend to voice his thoughts and create more tension.

"Thanks for agreeing to handle this situation," he said to break the silence. "We want to keep things as quiet as possible."

"And move things along quickly, right?" Alison added.

"Yes." His gaze met hers and he saw a spark of anger in her eyes, but he didn't understand why. Was she angry he'd embarrassed her in front of her fiancé?

"I'm glad to be able to help my daughter," Alison's mother said, sounding sincere. "Let's order and we'll discuss details while we eat."

They spent an exorbitant amount of time studying the menu. Alison ordered chicken salad, her mother the Caesar salad, while Brady opted for a club sandwich. Then both women toyed with their napkins, straightening and making sure they were folded just right—all time-killers, he realized. He contemplated Janelle Hartwell's return and wondered how it had affected Alison. Once upon a time, he would have asked her, but now...

Ice clinked in Janelle's tea as she squeezed lemon into it and stirred. "Now, tell me about yourself, Brady."

"Excuse me?"

"Alison told me you two met in high school. Are you the same age?"

He shook his head. "No, I was a senior when she was a freshman."

"So you dated your senior year, then you went to college?"

"Janelle—"

Alison's mother raised a hand. "I just want to get a feel for the whole situation. A divorce is a serious issue, you know."

"But we didn't know we were still married until two days ago," Alison protested.

Janelle gestured toward them with uplifted hands. "But you loved each other when you said your vows?"

Brady took a sip of his coffee, almost scalding his tongue. He hadn't been prepared to discuss his feelings for Alison with her, much less her mother. "Well, yes."

Alison's mother glanced at Alison, who nodded.

"And you pronounced those vows in a church?"

They both nodded.

Janelle narrowed her eyes. "Brady, Alison said you consummated the marriage?"

Heat climbed Brady's neck. "Yes."

"Mother, I don't understand. My goodness, you and Daddy got divorced, so why—"

"I'm just clarifying things." Janelle picked at her salad. "Now, it's true you both thought the marriage had been annulled the day after the ceremony?"

Again, they both nodded.

"So you believed you were free to be with other people?"

Brady swallowed, his jaw clenching as he looked at Alison. She squirmed and avoided eye contact.

"True?" Alison's mother asked. "Brady?"

"Well, yeah," Brady admitted.

"Alison?"

"I suppose so," Alison said quietly, staring at her water glass as if she wanted to jump in it and drown.

"And have either of you remarried during that time?"

"No," they both replied at once.

"How about affairs? Have you been involved with other people?"

Alison's eyes flickered with anger. "Mother, I don't think these questions are necessary."

"Adultery would constitute grounds for divorce," Janelle said matter-of-factly.

Alison squared her shoulders. "But we're going to do an uncontested—"

"Alison's engaged," Brady said, frowning over his sandwich.

"What?" Alison's fork clattered against the plate. "Who told you that?"

"Vivica. She said that that Eberson guy—"

"Emerson." Alison gave him a venomous look. "And we're not engaged."

"But Vivica—"

"He proposed. I told him I needed time."

"But you've..." Brady waved his fork around. "You've been together."

Alison leaned over the table, her voice a low hiss. "We haven't slept together!"

Something evil unleashed itself in Brady: relief.

Alison seemed to recognize the effect. Maybe because he was smiling.

Retribution darkened her eyes. "So what about you, Brady?"

"Me?"

"Yes, you? How many women have you been with?"

He should have known she'd turn the tables on him.

He glanced at Janelle, surprised at the way she was watching them both, as if they were performing some kind of show and she had a front row seat.

"Alison was honest," Janelle said. "I think you owe her that much."

Brady threw down his napkin. "Oh, hell." He hated to admit it. Some macho, superstud Air Force pilot he was. His voice came out low, angry. "All right. I haven't been with anyone."

Silence rasped between them.

"Excuse me?" Alison said.

He leaned over the table, both elbows planted firmly. Their faces were so close he could smell the lilac-scented shampoo she used. He could almost touch her mouth. "You heard me. None."

She caught her bottom lip between her teeth. Was she fighting a smile?

"So, there has been no adultery involved. But you both say you want this divorce?" Alison's mother asked.

Brady stared at Alison and hesitated. Alison stared at him. He could have sworn she was hesitating. Then a cramp suddenly seized his leg, tightening every muscle he'd worked during therapy, reminding him of his scars and the accident, driving home all the reasons they could never be together. He ground his teeth, determined to walk away without revealing the extent of his pain. Alison might have fond memories of them, but she wouldn't want the man he'd become, and he didn't want her pity.

"Yes, we're different people than we were four years ago," he said in a gruff voice, trying to stretch his leg beneath the table so he could stand. He had to go to the rest room and massage the knot. "I want the divorce. File the papers as soon as possible."

BRADY'S WORDS KNIFED through Alison. She hadn't realized she'd been hoping Brady would contest the divorce, that he would fight for her and their marriage.

"Alison?" Her mother's voice sounded soft, her touch light as she swept a hand over her daughter's.

Alison dragged her gaze from Brady, a quiver starting deep inside her that threatened to erupt any second. Dammit, she'd cried for months when he'd stopped writing her, then for months more when he'd started returning her letters. She refused to cry in front of him and her mother.

"Yes, Janelle. Go ahead and start the paperwork."

"I have a month's leave," Brady said, pushing to his feet, his expression harsh. "Hopefully, we can get everything signed before I have to report back."

Alison nodded, afraid to speak again as he excused himself to go to the men's room. His shoulders were thrown back, his head held high, his face hard as he walked away.

She knotted the napkin in her lap. The next month couldn't go by fast enough, she thought, feeling a wave of anguish. Then Brady Broussard would be out of her life forever.

Chapter Seven

Brady paced across the men's room, trying to walk out the cramp, but the muscles in his calf were so knotted that his leg buckled and he doubled over in pain. He knew the session with Vivi had been tough, but he hadn't been prepared for the exhaustion or the agony he'd feel afterward.

As much as he hated to give in to it, he was going to have to go home and do as Vivi had ordered—rest.

God, he hated it. Hated to be weak, hated this powerless feeling.

But first, he'd have to face Alison and her mother again and say a polite goodbye.

Tacking on his military face, he sucked in a harsh breath, pushed his body to attention in spite of the pain and headed back to the table.

ALISON HADN'T HAD TIME to recover from Brady's stark detachment when she glanced up and saw her sisters heading toward the table. They were both looking at her oddly, no doubt shocked to see her lunching with their mother.

Good grief, what was she going to tell them?

"Ali, what a surprise," Mimi said. She started to bend over to hug her, but her protruding stomach bumped the table and they both laughed.

"Hey, sis. Mom." Hannah's quiet voice mirrored the wariness in her eyes.

"Hi, girls." Janelle Hartwell's face flushed. "It's so nice to see you all here. Alison and I ran into each other and decided to eat together."

Alison's surprised gaze swung to her mother, but Janelle simply smiled and pretended normalcy, when nothing about their meeting had been normal. Making matters worse, Brady marched toward them, looking glum and serious, as if he'd received a death sentence.

"Actually, Brady and I were having lunch," Alison said, trying to gather her wits. "We met to discuss Vivica's wedding."

Hannah's raised eyebrow implied disbelief, while a mischievous grin tugged at Mimi's mouth.

"So what are you two up to?" Alison asked.

"I just came from my checkup," Mimi said, placing a protective hand over her belly.

"Is everything okay?" Alison asked.

"Doing great," Mimi said. "I'm hot, but fat and happy."

"She and the baby are in perfect health," Hannah said with a grin. "As long as she stays close by the next few weeks, we're in good shape."

Mimi frowned. "But I have to go visit Grammy Rose before the baby comes."

"I don't know." Worry furrowed Hannah's brow. "Sugar Hill doesn't have an emergency service set up to reach the mountains, and you're getting close to your due date.''

"I heard the town council discussing the emergency service last week," their mother said.

Hannah nodded. "Mayor Stone offered his support, and so did George Frost, who runs the flying service. The county's looking into buying a helicopter and utilizing one or two of the planes for medical emergencies.''

"Sounds like a great idea." Alison turned to Brady. "With your experience, you could probably give them some advice.''

Hannah jumped on the possibility. "Oh, Brady, would you?''

Brady stood ramrod straight, but Alison detected panic in his eyes. "I don't know. I'm not going to be here long.''

"I thought you were considering staying," Alison said.

"I'm on temporary leave, but my enlistment time isn't up." He frowned at her. "And right now I'm helping Mother out at the print shop.''

"Well, think about it," Hannah said. "The town could use someone experienced to advise them.''

"Look, I have to go now," Brady said. "I told Mother I'd come by and help her this afternoon.''

"Sit down and finish your sandwich, Brady," Janelle suggested. "The girls can join us, too.''

"We have a table over there." Hannah pointed to the corner.

"And I need to go. Just let me know what else I can do to help with Vivi's wedding." Brady angled his head to the side so only Alison could hear. "And let me know when the divorce is final."

Alison clenched her napkin tightly, tempted to hurl it at him as he turned and walked away. Yeah, he probably wanted to know the moment he was free, so he could go celebrate.

BRADY'S ENTIRE BODY ACHED as he left the restaurant, his heart a throbbing muscle that might quit ticking from the pain of leaving Alison. Although he'd planned to drive home, once again he found himself sidetracked, this time taking the Thunderbird by George Frost's airline service. Brady didn't intend to get involved, he told himself, he was simply curious about the small airport. Wiley Hartwell and other small-business owners used the private planes for work-related travel. Sugar Hill might be only a small dot on the map, but slowly the town was trying to update itself to the present.

The small airport, about thirty miles outside Sugar Hill, occupied several acres. Five planes sat in various plane ports, two smaller hangars held Cessnas—a 172 and a 182—and at the end, two larger hangars appeared vacant. One of them could easily house a helicopter for medical flight purposes.

He parked along the side of the dusty highway, angling the car so he could watch the runway. But business must be slow, because there was a lack of activity inside the gate. Nothing like the Columbus AFB where he'd first received his flight training and his first taste of the inside of a cockpit, or Davis Monthon AFB in Tucson where he'd trained.

A taste he'd thought he'd never be able to live without.

He climbed out of the car, walked to the gate and stared at one Cessna, remembering the first time he'd gotten behind the controls. His dad, who had been in the reserves, had rented a Cessna 152 and taken him up in it. Brady had been only six, hadn't even been able to see out the front window, but his dad had let him sit up front, and he'd explained the instruments to him. Brady had been so excited he'd almost wet his pants.

He'd decided then he would be a pilot like his dad. He craved the freedom of soaring through the air, the exhilaration.

Steady hands, his father had said. A man had to have steady hands and steady nerves to fly.

Now Brady had neither.

He held out his hands, and saw that they were trembling just like his insides. Josh's face flashed into his mind, the explosion, the spiraling plane, the crash, the scent of burning metal and flesh.

No, Brady's taste for flying had changed, just as the rest of his body had changed with the accident. Bitter memories now tainted the flavor, just as sweet memories of Alison stifled his attraction to any other woman.

ALISON STRUGGLED through the rest of the day, forcing herself to put on a cheerful facade for her customers. Finally, she closed the shop, picked up a carton of chocolate chip ice cream and headed home. She spent ten minutes in the shower cursing the heat; ten more cursing Brady Broussard; five more cursing herself for still caring about the blasted man while she tugged on boxers and an oversize T-shirt; then five more minutes staring at the hope chest. It was so beautiful, yet it had already brought so much turmoil into her life.

It wasn't the hope chest, she told herself as she grabbed a spoon and dragged herself to the TV, it was the contents. Those insufferable annulment papers. And Brady Broussard!

The stubborn, hardheaded, detached military man.

If he was so detached, though, why had he looked so stricken at the idea of advising the town on the medical flight service?

He hadn't, she told herself, dipping into the ice cream with a vengeance. He'd simply been stricken at the idea of spending time with her. She'd barely swallowed her first bite of ice cream when the doorbell rang. She glanced down at her sloppy clothes and messy hair and cursed again. It had better not be Brady or Thomas.

No, her nosy sisters stood on the doorstep, looking curious and determined.

Mimi took one look at the ice cream carton. "Okay, I knew something was up."

Hannah lifted a plastic bag, shrugging when Alison saw a carton of her other favorite flavor, Rocky Road.

"Comfort food," Mimi joked as she grabbed two more spoons from the kitchen drawer. They gathered around the coffee table, sharing both cartons.

"Okay, what gives?" Mimi smiled in ecstasy as she inhaled her first bite.

Alison feigned innocence. "What do you mean?"

"Don't play dumb, Ali," Hannah said. "You, Mom, Brady? An interesting combination."

"It was just a coincidence."

"We're not buying that," Mimi said.

"Too much tension," Hannah added.

Alison saw the love and understanding in her sisters' eyes, and tears welled up in her own.

"Oh, honey, what's wrong?" Hannah said.

Mimi reached out her arms. "Tell us, Ali."

Ali fought tears as memories of the past few days flashed through her mind. She wanted desperately to confide in her sisters, but both she and Brady had chosen her mother as their lawyer because they didn't want the entire town to know about the divorce. And Mimi and Hannah had a way of treating her like the kid sister. This was one problem she'd have to take care of herself. So she opted for a half-truth.

"I'm just so confused now. Having Mother around is really weird."

Her sisters frowned and mumbled agreement.

"And Thomas asked me to marry him, and now Brady Broussard shows up."

"It would be hard to choose between those two," Hannah admitted.

Mimi grinned mischievously. "Yeah, but what a choice."

"That's just it," Alison said. "I don't know what to do. Thomas is wonderful and sweet and so easy to get along with. And he'd make a great husband."

"And Brady?"

Alison shrugged and dug into the ice cream. "Brady is difficult and brooding and moody and…"

"Sexy?" Mimi supplied.

"That, too," Alison said, a tear trickling down her face.

Hannah handed her a box of tissues from the end table. "You still love him, don't you?"

"I...I can't," Alison wailed.

"Of course, you can," Mimi said. "That's the reason you couldn't say yes to Thomas's proposal—because your heart belongs to Brady."

"But Brady doesn't want me anymore."

Mimi reared up like a protective mother hen. "Did he tell you that?"

Alison nodded. What else could "file the divorce papers" mean?

Hannah and Mimi traded knowing looks. "Love isn't always easy," Hannah commented.

"Yeah, men can be a pain in the—"

Hannah frowned in warning.

"The butt," Mimi finished.

Alison crumpled the tissue, grabbed another and blew her nose. "Brady says we're different people, that we've changed. We're not foolish kids in love anymore."

Hannah winced. "Sounds like he's jaded."

"You might have to shake him up a little."

"What?"

Mimi giggled and wiggled her hips. "Shake him up a little. Use your sex appeal, Ali."

Hannah pointed to Mimi's swollen stomach. "Sex appeal is what got you into that condition."

Alison smiled. "Thanks, girls, but I'm not going to make Brady stay with me if he wants to move on."

Mimi sighed. ''Men don't know what they want. That's why they need women.''

Alison felt even more glum. ''Brady knows what he wants. He just doesn't want me.''

''So, what are you going to do?'' Hannah asked.

Alison summoned her courage. ''I'm going to give him exactly what he wants.'' *A divorce. Then I'll make myself fall in love with an easygoing guy like Thomas.*

Chapter Eight

The next day Alison waved at Mimi as she and Vivica walked into Sugar Hill's Hotspot.

Vivica sighed. "Mimi makes the best chocolate-chocolate chip muffins in the world. I could eat a dozen of them."

Alison laughed. "I know. I'd probably weigh two hundred pounds if I worked here."

"You're in great shape, Ali. I saw the way my brother was giving you the eye."

Alison blinked to control her reaction. "I swim every morning to keep in shape, and your brother wasn't giving me the eye."

"Oh, come on, Ali, I still think something's going on between you two."

Yeah, a divorce.

"Hey, girls, want some café mochas or a cappuccino while we go over the menu for the reception?"

"Sounds great," Vivica said. "I'll take a mocha."

"Decided to forget losing the five pounds, huh?"

Vivica grinned and shrugged. "Yeah, Joe told me he hated bony women."

"Good for him." Alison commandeered a table in a corner, away from the hubbub. The café was filled with people on their way to work, and early-morning shoppers who'd dropped by for coffee and lingered to browse through the book department. Alison spotted her cousin Rebecca talking with a customer and waved. So far, the Hotspot had done well, thanks to Mimi's desserts and Rebecca's savvy with books. And Alison couldn't forget Wiley's unique advertising.

Vivica helped Mimi bring over the tray, laden with their coffees and a sampling of pastries, including chocolate chip muffins. Vivica immediately snatched one.

"Want some of those at the reception?" Mimi asked with a giggle.

"I was thinking of having the entire wedding cake made out of the batter."

They all laughed and Mimi spread out her ideas for the menu. "The groom's cake isn't always traditional. How about we make it the chocolate-chocolate chip?"

"That's a wonderful idea," Vivica exclaimed.

"And we'll serve crab and shrimp appetizers—"

"And I want some of those swirly cheese sticks and spinach dip. Those are all Joe's favorites."

Alison's mind wandered as the other women discussed the food selections. What would she serve at her own wedding?

Strawberries, steak kabobs, chocolate éclairs...

She frowned in disgust. No, she wouldn't serve any of those things. They were all Brady's favorites.

She had to forget about Brady's preferences and start learning Thomas's.

BRADY SPENT THE MORNING working in the print shop, finishing up materials for a professor's presentation on careers for students at a local junior college.

Since his own career was up in the air, maybe he should attend, he mused.

"Brady, hon, Vivi and Alison are stopping by to check those invitations. You ran a few samples, didn't you?"

He nodded. "I'll get them."

Wading through the stacks of papers and orders to be picked up, he finally located the box and pulled an invitation out to check it himself.

Mrs. Inez Broussard requests the honor
of your presence at the wedding of her
son, Brady Broussard,
to
Alison Leigh Hartwell.
August 4, 2000
6:00 p.m.
Sugar Hill Chapel.

Good Lord! What a Freudian slip! He'd entered the correct date and time, but he'd typed in the wrong names.

Vivica was going to kill him. And what if Alison saw the invitation?

He had to do something fast.

But the door opened and in walked his sister and soon-to-be ex-wife.

Brady stuffed the invitation in the box and crammed it under the counter. He'd run them through the shredder later. Now he had to stall.

Vivica waved. "Hey, Brady, we dropped by to check the invitations."

He glanced from his sister to Alison, drinking in the sight of her. A pale pink blouse hugged her subtle curves, and tailored white slacks fit her trim body. Although she appeared professional, she reminded him of a strawberry ice-cream cone he wanted to devour.

Only she wasn't smiling or even making eye contact with him.

After the way they'd parted yesterday, he shouldn't have expected her to act differently, but it still hurt to have her look right past him as if they'd never shared an intimate moment in their lives.

"The invitations need to go out this week," Alison said in a businesslike voice. "If we can just check them, Vivi can make sure everything's correct."

He cleared his throat. "I'm sorry, Vivi, but the printer went haywire and smeared the ink. I just got the problem repaired. I'll run some copies and bring them when I come to therapy."

Vivica frowned. "Well, okay, I guess."

Alison nodded. "Call me if there's a problem, Vivi."

Then she turned and left without acknowledging him. Brady stared after her, his heart lurching.

"You should try and make up with her," Vivica said.

He glared at her. "There would have to be something between us in order for us to make up. Besides, you said she was dating that doctor."

"So?"

"So, nothing. It's over."

Vivica shook her head. "You're not fooling me, Brady. And I don't understand why you'd throw away a chance for happiness with someone as great as Ali."

Brady ignored her and took the box to the shredder. But he hesitated, then stuck one of the invitations in his pocket. No, Vivica wouldn't understand it, not unless he explained. And he didn't intend to. Not even when she tortured him during therapy sessions.

ALISON WAS GRATEFUL to have her business as a distraction. She had four weddings in July, then Vivica's the beginning of August, and a thousand details to take care of for each. When she hung up the phone at five o'clock, her head was pounding. The bridesmaids' dresses for Amy Davenport's wedding, which were already two weeks late, had finally come in, but they were all the wrong sizes, and bright pink instead of pale green. Administrators at the park reserved for Judy Butler's outdoor wedding had called to tell Alison a softball tournament for Little Leaguers had been scheduled that same day. And the reception hall where Beth Dupree was getting married next week had just been quarantined for some weird kind of bacteria growing in the walls that had made dozens of Girl Scouts sick with diarrhea the day before.

The phone pealed and Alison hissed. "This had better not be another emergency." She sucked in a deep breath and answered the phone. "Weddings to Remember, Alison Hartwell."

"Oh, my gosh, Miss Hartwell, you won't believe what's happened!"

"Who is this?"

"Denny over at Fancy Flowers. It's just awful, I don't know what we're going to do! Aphids have eaten all our boutonnieres for tomorrow!"

Alison dropped her head in her hands. "Oh, my gosh." The bride certainly didn't want her wedding to be memorable because bugs were crawling all over the groomsmen.

Ten minutes later, she'd calmed Denny, and they'd solved the problem by ordering from another florist in Atlanta. Denny was miffed about his loss, but the wedding had to go on.

Alison stepped outside, on her way home, when she heard the slight roar of an engine and looked up to see a small plane soaring above her. She'd never once seen a plane in the sky that hadn't made her think about Brady.

As she walked the two blocks to her flat, she remembered the letter he'd written about his first flight and his excitement.

Dear Alison,
God, baby, you won't believe what a day. It finally happened—I got my wings. Yep, after all these months, I finally got to crawl into the

cockpit of a fighter jet and really take her up. It was so much better than I'd imagined, and I've imagined it a lot, ever since I was six. I wondered if all that basic training stuff, all those boring lectures and manuals, the crap from the sarge, the simulator flights, were all worth it. But they were. I was soaring in the clouds, my hands on the controls, the engine humming, and it felt so right, like I knew just where I belonged.

I wish I could see you, Ali, and take you up with me. We'd ride in the clouds and I'd show you everything I've learned. Then we'd fly down to our spot at the lake and make love all night long. Sometimes when I'm lying in my bunk at night, I close my eyes, and I swear I can hear your voice whispering my name. And if I try really hard, I can hear you moaning like you did that night we made love. The purr of the engine today reminded me of that sound, and now every time I hear it, I think about you.

Love always,
your Brady

Alison blinked back tears as she remembered Brady's comment about staying in Sugar Hill and running the print shop. Even if he didn't want her anymore, he couldn't give up flying. He'd be miserable. As soon as she got home, she had to call Vivica and tell her to talk to him.

THE THERAPY SESSION had been brutal. He preferred the morning sessions to late afternoon, but he was trying to accommodate Vivica's schedule. Brady soaked in a hot bath, gradually feeling the tightness in his muscles dissipate and the pain in his body recede to a more tolerable level. Unfortunately, the pain of losing Alison would probably never leave him.

Shaking off the self-pity, he dried himself off, dragged on a pair of shorts and decided to settle on the patio to enjoy the late evening breeze with a Scotch, his alternative to the pain pills the doctor had prescribed. One drink wouldn't knock him out, but the medication would.

He poured a small shot and turned to open the balcony doors, almost tripping over his duffel. The stack of letters Alison had written him poked out the open top. Unable to resist, he grabbed a handful, carried them with him and sat down. He'd read them once more, but when the divorce was final, he'd pack them away forever, with all his memories and dreams.

Dear Brady,

I just got back from out first football game and had to write you. We lost seven to nothing, and I couldn't help but think that if you'd been on the field, we would have kicked their butts. I used to love to watch you play quarterback. All the girls did. You looked so handsome in that uniform, all those muscles rippling and that serious game face on. Now I lie in bed at night and imagine you in your Air Force uniform, and I bet you look twice as handsome, twice as strong. My hero. I miss you so much that sometimes I look out into the crowd and think I see you, then realize I'm only daydreaming, that you're hundreds of miles away. But Brady, you're never far away in my heart. I light a candle for you in my window every night and whisper a prayer that you'll come back to me safe and sound. That one day I'll feel your lips kiss me again, that one night I'll wake to find you in my bed.

The lights will be low, the candlelight flickering on your naked body, your muscles bunching as you strain above me. My body tingles all over just thinking about your hands exploring the sensitive spots you kissed that first night we made love. Secret places that no one has ever touched or kissed before. Places no one but you will ever see or feel. And you'll smile and grow hard against me, your body tensing when you realize that I've been naked, lying in bed for hours, just waiting for you.

Only you, Brady, it will always be only you.
I love you forever & ever & always,
Alison

Brady closed his eyes, letting Alison's words wash over him like a balm to his wounded soul. Those words had kept him alive while he'd been recovering in the hospital. Now he had to do the unselfish thing and release her from her promises, so she could find happiness with someone else.

ALISON WOUND THE PHONE cord around her finger. "Listen, Vivi, you have to talk to Brady. Make him realize he can't even think about staying here and taking over the print shop.''

''I agree. But what can I do?''

''Just keep pushing him to talk. Find out why he'd consider leaving the Air Force.''

Vivica sighed. ''I'll try, but I think you should be the one talking to him. I know he still cares about you, Ali.''

''No, he wants to move on, and that's okay.''

''What happened between you two?'' Vivica asked gently.

''We just grew up and went different ways,'' Alison said simply. ''I can accept it, but even if I'm not a part of his life, he'll never be happy here running a small business.'' She tucked a strand of hair behind her ear. ''I know he needs time to heal from his accident, but he has to miss flying. It's always been such a big part of him.''

''All right, all right, I'll talk to him.'' Vivica paused. ''Ali, are you sure you're going to be okay?''

Alison pasted on a brave face even though Vivica couldn't see her through the phone. ''I'll be fine.''

''What about Thomas?''

Alison closed her eyes and tried to imagine being married to Thomas. ''I...don't know right now, Vivi. I mean, he's wonderful and so nice, but...''

''But he's not Brady.''

Alison's throat clogged. She didn't even bother to reply.

BRADY HEARD A KNOCK on the door and tried to ignore it, but Vivica pushed through anyway. He glanced over his shoulder from the patio and glared at her. "Did you come to torture me some more?"

Vivica laughed softly. "I'm not pushing you to do anything you're not ready for."

Brady arched a brow. "You're worse than my lieutenant at flight training. Are you sure you didn't join the service while I was gone?"

Vivica folded her arms and laughed again as she leaned against the balcony rail. He watched her inhale the fresh evening air and thought how happy she seemed, how calm. She'd been a pretty wild teenager, but between college, her job and her new love interest, she'd definitely mellowed.

"What are you doing out here? Watching the stars?"

Brady nodded and tucked the letter beneath his leg. "Something like that."

Vivica turned to him, her gaze level. "You're not seriously considering staying here in Sugar Hill and taking over the family business, are you?"

Brady shrugged. "What if I was?"

Vivica frowned. "You'd be making a big mistake, Brady. I know how much you love the Air Force, how much you love flying—"

"I'm not going to discuss this with you, Vivi." He rose and limped inside, tucking the letter inside his T-shirt.

Vivica followed him. "Why not? What are you afraid of, Brady?"

He stiffened, anger churning through him. "I'm not afraid of anything. But I've grown up. Maybe I've decided the responsible thing to do is come back and help Mom."

"Mom can hire help if she needs it. She doesn't need you to be a martyr and give up flying—"

He swung around. "Vivi—"

"Alison is concerned, too, Brady."

"What the hell does Alison have to do with this?"

"She cares about you, you big idiot. I just got off the phone with her and she's worried—"

"I don't want Alison Hartwell's pity or concern."

"What happened between you two? You used to care about her."

"That was high school stuff, Vivi."

"But you wrote her for a while."

"Yeah, but I got tired of that and quit."

Vivica sighed. "If I'd known you'd stopped writing her, I'd have called her when you had the accident."

"I'm glad you didn't. I didn't want her pity then and I sure don't want it now."

"This isn't about pity, Brady, it's about your future. You love flying and I think you still care about Alison. I've seen the way you look at her—"

"I told you I'm not going to discuss this with you." He stared at her and pointed to the door. "Now, I'm tired, and if I'm going to make it through another one of your torture sessions tomorrow, I need to go to bed."

Vivica's mouth compressed into a tight line as she stomped out the door. Brady winced when she slammed it behind her.

Chapter Nine

Run, man, run! You have to save him.

Brady's own voice echoed inside his head. He shoved the rocks off of his leg and stood. But his leg buckled, refusing to cooperate. He cursed and dragged himself through the dirt toward the mangled plane, his heart pounding. The fire was like a hungry monster, consuming the plane, eating the metal and glass as if it were dry brush.

Josh! He tried to yell, but another explosion rent the air, drowning his voice. Flames burst from every part of the fighter jet. God, he had to hurry.

He grabbed the tip of the wing and crawled over it, scorching his hands and knees. He tore at the debris, pushed through the flames, calling Josh's name.

Then he saw his friend's face. Blood matted Josh's hair as he sat slumped over the controls. Fire licked along the walls of the cockpit. Flames danced around Josh, biting at his clothes. Brady yelled again and tried to push past them. But fire shot upward, surrounding Josh, consuming him. Brady could smell the burning metal, the blood....

He jerked awake, sweat soaking his hair and face, his body trembling. He stared at the empty room, the tangled sheets, the darkness, and dropped his face in his hands, silently screaming with rage. Why couldn't he have saved Josh?

Several minutes later, he crawled from bed, yanked on running shorts and a T-shirt and headed outside. He couldn't jog yet, but walking would be good for him. He had to think, to escape the demons.

Dawn crept around him as he trekked into the small sleepy town. Birds chirped, the smell of hot doughnuts and pastries wafted from the local bakery, a newspaper boy riding a bike tossed the morning edition on the dry front lawns. The sun shone brightly, but Brady felt dismal. Then he saw the rec center.

Was Alison inside, swimming laps as she used to early in the morning at the high school or had time changed her routine?

Telling himself he would only check out the weight room and get a drink of water, he pushed open the door. A full weight room sat to the left, another room with modern exercise equipment to the right. Signs to the locker rooms, a sauna, exercise classes, baby-sitting services and the swimming pool were posted in clear view. Unable to stop himself, he headed toward the pool.

Alison must have just arrived.

He stood in the shadows of the doorway, watching greedily as she tossed her gym bag on the floor, stripped off her T-shirt and shorts and began a series of stretching exercises. She wore a simple, one-piece navy suit that was split high on her thighs, showcasing those killer long legs. She was tanned and lean and more curvy than he remembered. Her breasts strained against the thin fabric of the suit as she raised her arms and stretched them above her head, and he swallowed, his pulse accelerating at the image.

Sweeping her long hair into a ponytail, she secured it with a rubber band, then executed a graceful dive into the water. The pool seemed to embrace her as she glided along, her long arms pulling her as if she put very little effort into the motions. But he knew she did. Her morning swims were a stress release, she'd told him, a time to think, to energize herself for the day. To burn calories so she could indulge in her favorite foods; she had a sweet tooth, a penchant for ice cream.

Funny how he hadn't forgotten the little things about her.

After several freestyle laps, she moved into a more serious workout, switching to the breaststroke, her specialty. The one she'd won the county championship with in high school. The water rippled around her in small waves, the outline of her body clear and perfect in the water. Brady felt himself growing aroused, not just by her beauty, but the calm confidence with which she executed the strokes.

Then suddenly she stopped. Turned over to her back. Gazed across the empty pool area and saw him in the doorway.

"Brady?"

He heard the catch in her voice. Damn. "I didn't mean to scare you."

"No, it's okay. But I thought I sensed someone watching me."

"I...I went for an early walk. I just happened by to check out the center."

She rolled into the backstroke and swam toward him. Knowing he'd look like a stalker if he didn't act casual, he moved across the deck, hesitating by the pool side.

She paused, placed both hands on the deck and leaned her chin on them, looking up at him. Her eyes raked over him from head to toe, her gaze pausing at his knee.

His mangled, scarred leg.

He instinctively shifted, his first instinct to turn and hide. He'd forgotten he was wearing shorts. It had been nearly dark when he'd left the house. Her lower lip quivered and he wanted to run, but that was impossible. He'd probably fall and make a big fool of himself.

Finally her gaze rose to his face and he braced himself, telling himself it was best she saw him the way he was now. Scarred and broken. Then she wouldn't want him.

"Why don't you come in? The water feels great."

Not what he'd expected. Her soft voice sounded damn near seductive echoing in the empty space. But she had to be putting him on; she didn't want to show him how repulsive she found him.

"I don't have a suit."

Her smile was slow and full of mischief. "I think those running shorts will suffice. Or you could go skinny-dipping like you did—"

As if she hadn't seen enough. "Alison, don't."

Her smile died. "What? Don't remind you of the good times?" A sad expression darkened her eyes. "We did have good times, Brady."

"I know." He hated the gruffness in his voice. "But those times are over."

She hesitated, licked her lips, smiled again, a beautiful come-hither look that made his gut wrench. Why was she acting this way, as if things hadn't changed, as if he was the same?

"They don't have to be."

His breath caught, but he remembered his conversation with Vivica. *Alison is worried about you....* Yeah, she was planning to marry Emerson, but she felt sorry for him. Brady didn't want any part of her sympathy.

"I have to go." He fisted his hands by his sides. "And, Alison, stay out of my business from now on."

"What?"

"I don't want you and my sister talking about me."

Disappointment and hurt flitted across her face, but he turned and walked toward the door. And this time he didn't try to hide his limp. He wanted her to remember exactly how bad his leg had looked so she'd know how much he had changed.

Just before he closed the door, she picked up a rubber flip-flop and threw it at him. "If you don't want me, Brady, then don't come back here and watch me swim again!"

He closed the door, heard the shoe bounce off of the surface, and promised himself he wouldn't.

"OF ALL THE NERVE!" Alison stepped from the shower and wrapped a towel around her body. "He is so infuriating!" She called Brady every vile name she could think of while she smoothed lotion on her legs, then dried her hair. She'd stopped by to work out and get up her nerve to finally tell Thomas they were finished.

She must be crazy. Thomas was easygoing, levelheaded, nice, consistent—the exact opposite of Brady. Yes, she must be crazy to consider calling it quits with Thomas.

But she was definitely finished with Brady Broussard.

The man had more moods than she did on a bad-hair PMS day. She did not need him screwing around with her head. One minute he was sneaking up on her and watching her swim, looking at her with lust and love in his eyes, the next he was staring at her in disdain and telling her to mind her own business. How dare the insufferable man!

If he'd been close enough, she'd have dragged him into the pool and clobbered him. Then she'd probably have tried to pound some sense into him. And then she would have tortured him with a hundred kisses. And after he was good and steamy from wanting her the way she'd wanted him a few minutes ago, she'd prance away, leaving *him* feeling hot and bothered and alone.

He couldn't play these games without being punished.

She halted, her bra half over her ear, one sock on, one off as she remembered the scars on his leg, the way he'd stiffened when he'd seen her look at them. Punishment…

Maybe Brady's idea to return to Sugar Hill and run his father's business, his idea to push her away—maybe it was a form of punishment. She yanked at her underwear, lost her balance and hopped around, trying to steady herself. But she tripped over her sneaker and fell *kaplunk* on the cold locker room floor, staring at her worn-out shoes. Could Brady be feeling so guilty about the accident he'd decided to punish himself by giving up the thing he loved most—flying?

And what about her? No, she wouldn't entertain the idea that he still loved her. Oh, he still wanted her sexually, that much was obvious, but love—no, Brady had obviously forgotten what love meant.

It didn't mean driving someone crazy.

But the part about flying, about punishing himself—that made sense.

She blew her hair from her eyes, pushed herself up to finish dressing, Brady's last words screeching in her head like a siren. *Stay out of my business. I don't want you and my sister talking about me.*

Well, hell, she thought, fastening her bra with a snap. She'd never taken orders from a man before, and she certainly didn't intend to take them from Brady. Husband or not.

BACK AT HOME, Brady showered and changed, then hurried to the print shop before his mother arrived, determined to escape her doting and avoid another run-in with Vivica. Eight years on his own, almost four in the military, had ingrained independence in him, but his mother seemed to have forgotten he'd ever been away. He'd learned how to survive on nothing but the barest of rations, how to brave the wilds of the jungle and survive in enemy territory, yet yesterday his mother had started to cut his French toast for him. He'd had to politely take the cutlery before she offered to feed him like a baby.

But Alison hadn't coddled him. No, she'd looked at his scar, invited him to swim with her as if she'd actually *wanted* him, then thrown her shoe and yelled at him when he'd made her mad. He grinned, feeling almost normal again.

Ridiculous.

When he arrived at the shop, he turned on the lights and headed to his new desk, the one his mother had already fixed with his engraved nameplate, and began to sort through the day's list of tasks.

Judging by the stack on his desk, he had a full day's work. Exactly as he'd had the day before.

"THOMAS, I APPRECIATE you meeting me here." Alison sipped her diet soda to moisten her dry mouth. She'd practiced her speech a dozen times on the way to meet Thomas, but now the words stuck in her throat like glue.

Running into Brady earlier had really rattled her. Then she'd bumped into Vivica, who had pressed her to meet for lunch, wanting to discuss Brady. Alison had been so upset, she'd refused both.

To top that off, when she'd first entered the Hotspot, she'd seen her mother *and* father sitting in a booth together, talking and laughing. They were actually getting along.

Alison took another sip of soda, missed her mouth and sent cold cola trickling down her chin. Jerking herself back to her senses, she grabbed several napkins and tried to clean up the mess.

Thomas smiled and cradled his coffee between his hands. "What's going on, Ali? You seem nervous."

The sugar packets were spilling from the container at an odd angle so she straightened them. Thomas caught her hand and stilled her movements.

"Come on, we've been friends for a while now. Something's bothering you."

"I can't marry you right now." Alison closed her eyes, hating herself for simply blurting it out.

"I know."

She jerked her eyes open. "What?"

His smile was so understanding she wanted to cry. "I know. It's that Broussard guy that came back to town, isn't it?"

She opened her mouth to deny it, but he arched a brow, and she paused. "Yes. No. It's complicated."

"Ahh."

"You really should be a shrink instead of an OB-GYN. You're such a good listener, Thomas."

"Most women rattle on when they get nervous. I have to do something while I'm examining them."

Alison glanced at his face, saw the teasing in his eyes and laughed. She reached up and hugged him. "Oh, Thomas, you're so understanding. I…just need more time. My life is crazy right now with so many weddings to plan and my mom coming back to town. But I do care about you.''

He traced a finger along her hairline, tucking a strand behind her ear. ''It's all right. There's no rush, Ali. Take all the time you want. I'll be here when you decide.''

Alison squeezed his hand and thought about the hope chest, the veil, the annulment papers. Could they be signs suggesting she free herself to be with Thomas?

He leaned over and kissed her cheek. ''Let me know when you work things out, okay?''

''I promise.'' She squeezed his hand and watched him go, confusion washing over her. Darn it, why couldn't Brady be as easy to understand and get along with as Thomas?

She glanced across the bookstore. Maybe Rebecca could help her find a good how-to book on men— how to understand the husband you didn't realize you still had. Or how to love the man you *should* love, and forget the ones who'd already broken your heart. Out of the corner of her eye, she spotted her father rising. Probably going to check on Mimi, who was pregnant and happy and as rosy as a big ripe strawberry.

Instead her dad headed straight for her.

Uh-oh, she was in for it now. From the fierce fatherly expression on her dad's face, she had a feeling her mother had told him about the divorce.

VIVICA STORMED INTO the print shop and slammed a fist on the counter. ''What in the world did you do to Alison?''

Brady dropped the shipment of fliers he'd just completed, sending them scattering all over the floor. "Dammit, Vivi, look what you made me do."

"You did something to upset her and I want to know what."

"What makes you think I did something to her?" Irritation crawled over Brady. The fliers were probably dirty and he'd have to reprint them, as if the first time hadn't been boring enough. He tried to kneel to salvage them, but pain knifed through his leg, and he wobbled and broke out in a sweat.

"Good grief, Brady, I'll get the stupid fliers." Vivica ran a hand through her pixie hair, spiking the ends. "You get us some coffee, because we're going to talk—"

"But—"

"No buts about it." She wagged a red fingernail at him that was so long it could be ranked as a lethal weapon. "I'm not leaving here until I get an answer."

Brady limped back to the small break room, poured them each a cup of coffee and sat down at the table, massaging the pain away as best he could and trying to think of some way to appease his sister. Vivica stormed in a minute later, her hands on her hips, her head wobbling from side to side, she was so angry. He wondered if Joe had witnessed her temper yet.

"All right, spill it, Brother."

Brady's stomach balled into a knot. "Why do you think I did something to Alison?"

"Because I saw her after her morning swim and she was upset."

"She was?"

"Yes. I've never seen her so agitated. And when I mentioned you, I thought her blood pressure was going off the charts. What in heaven's name did you do?"

Brady shrugged. Maybe he'd finally pushed her away for good.

"Either spill it or the next physical therapy session will make the others look like a picnic."

Oh, hell. He might as well confess. When Vivica got something in her head, she'd never let it go. She'd drive her husband crazy.

She tapped her foot on the floor. "Brady?"

"Okay, you want to know what's going on between me and Alison?"

"Yes, and you'd better tell me the truth."

He nodded, resigned. Obviously Alison hadn't told his sister about their marriage. The realization stung. "All right, Vivi. You're right, I did have a thing for Alison years ago."

"I know that. Heck, *everyone* knew it."

Heat scorched his neck. He hadn't realized he'd been so obvious. "Well, what you don't know is that I married her."

Chapter Ten

"You did what?" The chair clattered as Vivica fell into it.

"I married her." Brady studied his hands, then finally met Vivica's wide eyes.

"When did this happen? Since you came back?"

He shook his head and explained about their hasty ceremony the night before he'd shipped out for training.

"You've been married for the past four years?"

He nodded.

"How romantic, Brady."

He shrugged. "Yeah, well, we were young and impulsive—"

"And in love." Vivi sighed dreamily, clasping her hands together. "And you still are, aren't you? After all these years of being apart—"

"You didn't let me finish." He cleared his throat. "Alison's father found out that night and hit the roof. He insisted we get the marriage annulled."

"Oh, so you aren't still married?"

"Actually, we are."

Vivica was sitting on the edge of the chair now. He'd never seen her so quiet. "I don't understand."

He explained about the hope chest and annulment papers. "Apparently Alison's grandmother forgot to file the papers."

"So you're still married." Vivica broke into a smile. "Brady, that's wonderful!" She jumped up and hugged him, oblivious to his turmoil.

He stiffened in her arms, took her by the shoulders and set her back. "No, honey, it's not. We're filing for a divorce."

"A divorce?"

"Shh, we don't want everyone to know," Brady said.

Vivica's eyes widened. "But why?"

"Because everyone will talk, and Alison's concerned about her reputation as a wedding coordinator—"

"No, I mean why are you getting a divorce?"

"Because…" he ran his hand through his hair "…because we've grown up and changed and—"

Vivica grabbed his arm. "That's ridiculous. You still love her and I know she loves you!"

He stood, nearly knocking over his chair, and crossed the room to the window. "She's marrying that Emerson guy."

"No, she's not."

"She's not?"

"I don't think so. But now I understand why she's so upset." Vivica stalked toward him. "You asked for this divorce, didn't you?"

"Well, yes."

"You big, stupid, stubborn oaf!" She swatted

him with her purse. "You came back and thought she'd found someone else and got jealous and gave up."

He covered his head to ward off another blow. "I'm not jealous!"

Her eyes crinkled with disbelief. "So you didn't mind seeing her with Thomas?"

"Of course I minded, but—"

"See, you are jealous, because you still love her."

"It's not like that."

She batted him again. "Yes, it is—"

"Listen, Vivi, I'm not the same man she married. For God's sake, look at me."

He caught her hands and made her stop and really look at him. "I can barely walk, much less jog anymore. I'm on medical leave from the Air Force pending an evaluation over whether or not I'll be able to return to active duty. I don't know what my future holds, I'm—"

"You're using your medical condition as an excuse."

"What?"

"You are, Brady Broussard. You're embarrassed about a few silly scars and you're using them as an excuse not to be with the woman you love."

"You're wrong, Vivi." Brady turned and leaned against the counter, suddenly exhausted as the burden of his guilt weighed down on him. "It's a lot more than that. A whole lot more."

Vivi placed a hand on his shoulder, her voice softening. "Then tell me what's wrong, Brady."

He squeezed his eyes shut, the image of Josh's

body lying in the charred rubble of the plane flashing in his mind. The image was so vivid bile rose to his throat.

"You have to get over feeling sorry for yourself so you can move on," Vivica said.

Brady glared at her. "You don't know what you're talking about, Vivi."

"I know this—if you give up Alison without fighting for her, you'll be making the biggest mistake of your life. And if you give up the flying, you're not the Brady I've always known." Vivica threw up her hands and stormed toward the door. "And we all want the old Brady back."

Brady tossed his cup in the trash without bothering to reply.

After all, she didn't want to hear what he would say—that the old Brady was never coming back. Because the old Brady had died in the crash that had killed Josh.

ALISON GATHERED HER WITS while her father dumped half a container of sugar in his coffee, rolled up the sleeves of his flowered shirt and settled into the seat across from her.

"Hey, cupcake."

"Hi, Dad."

He slurped his coffee. "How's the business?"

"Great. I've scheduled four weddings this month and I'm working on filling the August calendar now."

"Vivica's getting married in August, right?"

"Yes, Daddy. You know I'm planning her wedding."

"You're the maid of honor?"

"Actually, yes." She'd been so busy thinking about Brady she hadn't even thought about her own role in the wedding.

"You'll be beautiful, I know it." He broke off the edge of a cinnamon bun and bit into it.

"Dad, what's going on between you and Mom?"

Her father's eyebrows knitted together. "Nothing, hon. We're just trying to be friends. We decided we needed to be civil if we're going to live in the same town."

Alison nodded.

Her dad sipped his coffee. "I saw Brady at the parade the other day."

Alison squirmed. "Yes, he's back for a month." She explained about his accident, his temporary medical leave, the physical therapy.

Finally her father looked into her eyes. "Your mother told me about the divorce."

Here it comes. Did he think she and Brady had pulled something over on him? "Dad, Brady and I didn't know the annulment papers hadn't been filed until a few days ago."

"I realize that."

"Oh. Janelle shouldn't have told you. I told her I wanted this whole thing to be kept quiet."

"Honey, your mom cares about you and was worried."

Alison fiddled with her napkin. "Did you know Grammy hadn't filed the papers?"

Her father chuckled. "Nope, but I'm not surprised."

"Why? Was she having trouble remembering things?"

Her dad laughed again. "Hardly. Your grandmother is the most lucid woman I know. But she's also the most stubborn, thinks she knows everything."

Alison leaned her cheek in the palm of her hand. "I don't understand, Dad."

"I think she didn't file them because she didn't want to." He wolfed down another bite of the cinnamon bun. "See, your grandmother disagreed with me about the annulment. She thought I was wrong to push you into it."

Alison's mouth gaped open. "Really?"

"Yep." Her dad wiped icing from his chin. "I've been thinking lately, wondering if I made a mistake that day."

Alison frowned. "I never thought I'd hear you say that."

Her dad reached over and squeezed her hand. "I saw you with that baby doctor. Mimi said he asked you to marry him."

Alison winced, wondering if he wanted her to marry Thomas. "I told him I needed time, Dad."

"Because you still love Brady?"

"Dad—"

Her father held up his hand. "Look, hon, I know it's none of my business. And I'm sorry for the way things happened four years ago. It caused a rift between us and I've always worried about that."

Alison's throat clogged at the misery in her father's face. "Dad, I know you did what you thought was best. Brady and I were young and we got carried away.''

He pushed away his plate, shifting restlessly, his face ruddy. ''But sometimes that one person comes along, and if you don't grab them right then, you can lose them forever.''

Like she was doing right now with Brady. ''But if it's real love it lasts forever, Dad.''

''For better or worse. Remember that when you and Brady sit down to sign those divorce papers.''

Confusion filled Alison's head. What exactly was her father trying to say? Was he suggesting they shouldn't go through with the divorce?

''BRADY, a couple of your old friends are here to see you,'' his mother chirped.

Brady looked up from the computer in surprise. ''Johnny, Bobby Raye, it's been a long time.''

Johnny, a hulking ex-linebacker for his old high school team, pumped his hand. ''Hey, man, we heard you were back.''

Bobby Raye, a former member of the wrestling team, grabbed him in a hug. ''Yeah, we didn't expect to find you here, though.''

Brady shrugged. ''I told my mother I'd help her out while I was here.'' He gestured toward the wooden chairs in the office, and his friends sat. Except for a few gray hairs, Johnny still looked in pretty good shape, even in his dull-gray work uniform, but Bobby Raye had added about fifty pounds, mostly in the form of a beer gut.

''So, how long are you here for?''

"I have a month's leave. Wanted to be here for my sister's wedding." Brady explained about the accident, omitting the details.

"We were hoping you'd go with us for a beer." Bobby Raye checked his watch. "It's five o'clock, quitting time."

"Yeah, Pinto's Pug has ninety-nine cent drafts till seven," Johnny added, already standing.

Brady considered declining, but decided it would be nice to catch up on his old friends' lives. After all, if he decided not to reenlist, to stay in Sugar Hill, he'd be seeing them often.

A few minutes later they were seated at the smoky bar, ice-cold drafts and a bowl of peanuts in front of them. A pool room occupied the back corner, a dart game the right, and a big-screen TV blared in the background.

"Is this your regular hangout?" Brady asked.

"Most of the guys come here to watch the sporting events," Johnny replied.

"So, tell me what you guys have been up to since college," Brady said.

Both his friends shrugged. "Me and Wanda split again," Bobby Raye said. "She's just a nag. Don't appreciate how hard I work at the shop." He cracked a peanut shell with his teeth, then sucked down the contents. "Got this honey-do list a mile long. Wants me to come home and do this, do that, then crawl into bed and cuddle her." Bobby Raye patted his glass. "Sometimes a man just wants to kick back, watch the ball game and have a cold one, you know what I mean?"

Brady nodded, although he wasn't sure he did. Bobby Raye had planned to major in engineering. He'd once talked of building bridges in Europe. "Didn't you go into engineering like you planned?"

Bobby Raye shrugged and crushed another handful of peanuts in his fist. "Nah, dropped out after the first year. I work at my daddy's auto shop now."

"He does the best brake work in town," Johnny said, elbowing Brady. "Gives the best damn price, too. I take all my trucks there."

"Your trucks?" Brady frowned. "I thought you were going to study finance and make a million before forty."

Johnny shrugged. "Flunked out first semester. Too much partying."

Bobby Raye and Johnny laughed. "But he runs a great delivery service, even moving into that 'dot.com' stuff. And he's single, out with a different woman every night."

"Tell us what you've been doing, Mr. Air Force pilot." Johnny gave a low whistle. "All those things we talked about doing sort of slipped away, but you actually went out and did them."

"Yeah, you got guts," Bobby Raye said.

Brady frowned into his beer, remembering the way the three of them used to sit around and dream. The guys were right. He had gone out and chased his dream. Only now, he was considering giving it all up.

He glanced at both of them again, studying their faces. They seemed content, but would he be if he stayed here and took over his father's business?

ALISON TRIED TO ESCAPE the coffee shop without running into her mother, but her day seemed destined for family interference.

Her mother cornered her at the door. "Can we talk for a second?"

"Sure." Alison checked her watch. "But I have to meet a client in a few minutes."

Her mother smiled. "Okay, I just wanted you to know I filed the papers, so everything's underway."

Alison nodded. "I can't believe you told Dad about the divorce. Who else did you tell?"

"No one. And I'm sorry, honey, but he is your father and he cares a lot about you." She stroked Alison's shoulder. "If you ever want to talk, ever need someone to listen who might understand, I'm here."

"What?"

Her mother played with the gold chain around her neck, looking uncertain, surprising Alison more. "Look, honey, I know I haven't been around much—"

"You haven't been around at all for the last twenty-some years."

"Right." Her mother took a deep breath. "But I'm here now for you girls, and I'll help you any way I can."

"You're filing the papers. That's all I want from you."

Hurt flickered in her mother's eyes. "I know I deserve that, Alison, that I've been a terrible mother...."

Alison remained silent. She certainly couldn't argue with that.

"But I do understand the pain of a divorce, even if it's one you choose to have. There's a certain sense of failure, of sadness."

"You felt those things when you divorced Dad?"

"Yes." Janelle rubbed at her temple. "I've carried around a lot of guilt and a sense of failure for years. I don't want you to do that."

Alison bit her lip. She did feel a sense of failure.

"And I have to admit Wiley's been a wonderful father. I look at him now and admire him."

Alison was speechless. Her mother was actually complimenting Wiley, sounding as if she liked him. But she was right—her father had been wonderful, devoted and steadfast even when the girls had gone through awkward rebellious stages and tried to push him away.

The meeting with Brady came to Alison's mind, and the sense that he might be trying to punish himself. That he was pushing her away. It had been a long time since they'd spoken their vows. His accident, the therapy—this was definitely a rough time for Brady. Maybe he needed to know she would love him for better or *worse*.

Maybe her sense of failure was coming from not fighting hard enough, from giving up too soon.

"Alison, are you all right? You have a funny look on your face."

Alison looked at her mother and smiled. "Yes, I'm fine. But I have to go." She hurried through the doorway, adrenaline pumping through her. Maybe she should think of a plan, a way to get close to Brady again, to *show* him she loved him. After all, her divorce would be final on the same day Brady's sister got married.

She had less than three weeks to convince Brady they could have a future together.

Chapter Eleven

Brady awoke with a start. He'd had another nightmare.

But this time he hadn't dreamed about the crash. He stared into the predawn light, a mixture of relief and anxiety splintering through him.

Instead, he'd dreamed about staying at the print shop. He'd seen himself in five years, buried in paperwork, bored, irritable, thirty pounds heavier with a beer gut of his own, stopping by the Pug every day with Bobby Raye, dating an endless number of women, going nowhere in life. In the dream, he staggered out of the bar and saw Alison pregnant with another man's child.

Disgusted, he threw back the covers, climbed from bed and dressed in running shorts again. He stepped outside and drank in the fresh air.

Once again he found himself walking by the rec center. He'd promised himself he wouldn't watch Alison swim again, yet, after that dream, he had to see her.

She was swimming her laps, had already started the breaststroke, the peaceful silence accentuated by the occasional ripple of her arms brushing through the water. Today she wore a simple dark green suit that hugged her curves and dipped slightly lower in front to give a hint of cleavage. He stood in the shadows, his body hard at the sight of her. He ached to go inside the pool area, yet he held back. His sister was right—he wasn't the old Brady. He was a coward.

Too afraid to tell her the truth about himself, too afraid to see the disgust or disappointment in her eyes when he revealed his flaws.

"Brady?"

His breath caught at the sound of his name. Unable to help himself, he moved to the side of the pool and knelt. Alison propped her arms on the edge, water droplets glistening on her skin and hair, a soft smile on her face.

"I wish you'd join me."

He shook his head, unable to speak. Then she cupped his chin with her hand, pulled his face down and kissed him. He savored the sweetness of her lips, the subtle hunger in the throaty moan that escaped her when they finally pulled apart.

"I've missed you, Brady."

"I missed you, too," he heard himself admit.

She pressed her forehead against his, her breath whispering in the silence of the room. And he knew then that he didn't want to wind up like the man in his dreams. He missed the old Brady, and he wanted him back.

"I'll see you later?" she asked softly.

He nodded, drew in a deep breath, straightened

his aching leg, then turned and left, determined to face his demons.

ALISON FINISHED HER LAPS, confusion mingling with hope as she remembered the kiss, the gentle way he'd responded, the hungry need in his eyes when they'd pulled apart. She showered and dressed, contemplating the kiss along with everything Brady had said since he'd returned. He did still want her, at least on some elemental physical level. But would it be enough to bring them back together?

LATER, AT HOME, Brady showered and dressed, grateful for the progress he was making during the grueling therapy sessions. Although the doctor had said he would always have a slight limp, his leg was already feeling stronger, his limp seemed less pronounced.

He met his mother in the kitchen. She was already pouring his coffee. "Do you want to ride in together today?"

He froze, realizing how easily he'd let her take control of his life. It was time he took it back. If he wanted Alison to respect him, he had to respect himself first. Maybe Vivi had been right. Maybe he had been feeling sorry for himself. "No, Mom, I have something I need to do first. Do you think I could take Dad's old Durango?"

"Sure. I try to drive it once a week just to keep it running." She lifted a shaky hand to her cheek. "I keep telling myself I should sell it, but I just haven't been able to part with the thing."

His father had loved the old Durango, had taken

it up in the mountains for days at a time when he went fishing. Brady wrapped his arm around his mother's shoulders and hugged her, thinking of Alison's letters and how difficult it was to give up certain sentimental things.

Thirty minutes later, he sat outside the small airport, staring at the runway, watching as one of the pilots pulled his aircraft from a small plane port and gassed it up. Brady's heart beat double time, while adrenaline and the old familiar itch of excitement budded in his chest. Yet his hands trembled as he opened the car door and climbed out.

He walked to the larger hangar and stuck his head in. A tall thin man wearing coveralls threw up a hand. "Hi, there. What can I do for you?"

Brady introduced himself.

"Oh, right, you're Vivica's brother. She talks about you all the time. Told us what a hotshot pilot you are."

Used to be. "I was driving by and wondered if you'd mind if I looked around."

The man, who appeared to be in his forties, stuck out his hand. "Sure don't. Name's George. I run the flying service around here, got a few pilots that keep their planes here."

"Hannah Hartwell mentioned something about wanting to start a medical flight service here."

"Yeah, they're looking into buying a chopper. Gonna need someone who knows what he's doing to take it up in the mountains. Right now all we have are those Cessnas. They can't get in and out of places a chopper could."

"Right." Brady touched the Cessna's wing. The

metal felt cool and slick, comforting like an old friend.

"Check her out if you want. I need to talk to Daryl Sawyer before he takes off." He pointed to the other pilot, now preparing for flight, and Brady thanked him.

Pushing memories of the crash from his mind, he climbed inside the plane. Baby steps—wasn't that what the psychologist who'd evaluated him after the crash had said? She'd diagnosed him as having post-traumatic stress disorder and assured him he'd recover little by little. She'd told him talking about the accident would help rid himself of the guilt.

But he hadn't been able to do that. He'd bottled up his feelings until he felt like a bottle with a cork ready to blow.

But he was taking a step today. He moved into the cockpit and slid into the seat, breathing deeply to calm himself. He could do this; he could face his demons. And maybe he could actually fly again, someday.

He ran his hand along the seat, reached out to touch the control panel, but his fingers began to shake, his heart to pound. *You can do this. Get a grip.*

He rubbed his fingers along the radio, reviewed the checklist on the clipboard, remembering all the steps that needed to be checked before takeoff. He mentally went through those steps, checked the gas and looked out onto the runway.

Josh's face appeared in front of him, his eyes wide with fear, his hair matted with blood, fire lick-

Play **LUCKY HEARTS** for this...

exciting *FREE* gift!
This surprise mystery gift could be yours free

when you play **LUCKY HEARTS!**
...then continue your lucky streak with a sweetheart of a deal!

1. Play Lucky Hearts as instructed on the opposite page.

2. Send back this card and you'll receive 2 brand-new Harlequin American Romance® novels. These books have a cover price of $4.25 each in the U.S. and $4.99 each in Canada, but they are yours to keep absolutely free.

3. There's no catch! You're under no obligation to buy anything. We charge nothing—ZERO—for your first shipment. And you don't have to make any minimum number of purchases—not even one!

4. The fact is thousands of readers enjoy receiving their books by mail from the Harlequin Reader Service®. They enjoy the convenience of home delivery...they like getting the best new novels at discount prices, BEFORE they're available in stores...and they love their *Heart to Heart* subscriber newsletter featuring author news, horoscopes, recipes, book reviews and much more!

5. We hope that after receiving your free books you'll want to remain a subscriber. But the choice is yours—to continue or cancel, any time at all! So why not take us up on our invitation, with no risk of any kind. You'll be glad you did!

Visit us online at
www.eHarlequin.com

The Harlequin Reader Service®—Here's how it works:

Accepting your 2 free books and gift places you under no obligation to buy anything. You may keep the books and gift and return the shipping statement marked "cancel." If you do not cancel, about a month later we'll send you 4 additional novels and bill you just $3.57 each in the U.S., or $3.96 each in Canada, plus 25¢ shipping & handling per book and applicable taxes if any.* That's the complete price and — compared to cover prices of $4.25 each in the U.S. and $4.99 each in Canada — it's quite a bargain! You may cancel at any time, but if you choose to continue, every month we'll send you 4 more books, which you may either purchase at the discount price or return to us and cancel your subscription.

*Terms and prices subject to change without notice. Sales tax applicable in N.Y. Canadian residents will be charged applicable provincial taxes and GST.

ing at him. Brady coughed and let out a groan, voices echoing in his head.

"Pull up, pull up, you're too close to the mountain!"

"Something's wrong, man. I'm going down."

"Eject! Now, Josh!"

"I'm trying. The eject button's malfunctioning!"

The Cessna's windshield became a blur, the images of the crash reeling across it like a horror show on a movie screen. Brady dragged himself from the plane, leaning against its metal flank to get some air, nearly choking on the unshed tears clogged in his throat.

ALISON FELT DIZZY from the scents in the floral shop, almost as dizzy as she had this morning after her swim. She'd felt Brady's eyes on her, had known the moment he'd appeared. And she hadn't been able to stop herself from kissing him.

"Hello, Earth to Alison." Vivica waved her hand in front of Alison's face. "We were talking about the flowers."

"Oh, right. Sorry."

Vivica laughed. "That's okay, but I'd love to know what you were thinking. You had this really weird look on your face."

Alison picked a rose from the assortment on the counter and sniffed it. "What kind of look?"

"Like you were thinking of somebody." Vivica grinned. "A man. Maybe my brother?"

Alison laughed. "Don't be silly. How could you tell that from a look?"

"Your cheeks were flushed."

"They were not." Alison batted at her with the tip of the rose. "Now, choose your flowers so we can have lunch. I'm starved."

"Okay, but we will finish this discussion. I want to talk to you about Brady."

Alison opened her mouth to argue, but Vivica silenced her with a warning look. "I want yellow roses in my bridal bouquet, and how about the bridesmaids carry white?"

"That'll look great with the pale blue bridesmaids' dresses," Alison said. "We can add shades of green for accents. I'll have the florist make you a special throwaway bouquet so you can preserve the one you carry in the ceremony."

"Perfect." Vivica hugged her. "I never would have thought of that."

Alison helped Vivica place the order, suggesting she could save money by using fresh flowers for the reception, and Vivica agreed.

"The more money we'll have to spend on our honeymoon." She paused and grabbed Alison's hand. "You and Brady didn't take a honeymoon, did you?"

Alison nearly dropped her clipboard. "He told you?"

"Yes." Vivica chuckled. "Actually, I kind of dragged it out of him."

Alison blew out a shaky breath. "It was a long time ago."

"Not so long ago that you two don't still love each other."

"Vivi—"

"We're going to discuss this, Ali." Vivica pulled

her outside and they ducked into the Hotspot. Alison checked quickly, grateful her mother and father weren't around. They waved to Mimi, who sat huddled with Seth, having lunch. Seth had dozens of pamphlets of baby paraphernalia spread on the table, while Mimi cuddled a big yellow elephant Seth had obviously bought.

After they'd ordered sandwiches, Vivica began. "I had a major talk with Brady last night."

"And?"

"And he finally threw me out, but I think I hit a nerve. I think Brady's scared."

Alison gulped. "Of what?"

"Of you not wanting him because of the scars."

Leave it to Vivica to be up-front. "That's crazy. I don't care about a few scars."

"I know that and you know that, but my brother can be so stubborn. Did you want the divorce?"

"I don't know." Alison shrugged and explained. "When Brady stopped writing and then returned my letters without opening them, I assumed he'd met someone else. That he didn't want me anymore."

"That's not what happened."

"I know. He explained about the flight training, and now I know about the accident. But you should have heard him, Vivi. He said he wanted the divorce, that we weren't kids with silly dreams anymore. I won't cling to someone who doesn't want me."

"How about fighting for the man you love?"

Alison pressed a finger to her temple. "What if he doesn't love me anymore?"

"Then he's either a fool or the military is training

idiots.'' Vivica sighed and pressed her spoon against her tea bag. ''My theory is that he feels bad about the crash and he's blaming himself, and he's afraid you'll think he's...I don't know, less than he was before.''

Alison pushed her sandwich away, her appetite forgotten. ''That's crazy.''

''I know, but Brady does have that kind of macho man mentality.''

''You may have a point. I've been wondering if he thought he had to punish himself or something.''

''So, what are you going to do?''

Kiss him again and find out? ''I don't know, Vivi. But if I figure it out, I'll let you know.''

Vivica wiggled her finger. ''Come here. I have an idea. You know that thirty-day waiting period...?''

Alison twisted her mouth, wondering what her friend had in mind. Vivica always had had a sneaky side to her.

BRADY SHOWERED after his therapy session, every muscle in his body protesting. Instead of letting up, Vivica seemed to be getting tougher with each session.

''Come on, Brady. I want you to check out the chapel with me.''

''Why do you need me to go, Vivi? You and Alison can handle the details.''

''But Joe isn't here and I want a man's perspective.''

Brady ground his teeth and let her drag him to the car. Several minutes later, they parked by the lake, the fading afternoon sunlight spilling onto the small, old-fashioned white chapel, the water lapping softly at the bank. Alison was standing on the front stoop in a white sundress, with her dark hair brushing her shoulders. She looked like some sort of angel, and as he approached, he inhaled the scent of lilacs. His body automatically tensed.

"We'll do a quick walk-through and decide what kind of decorations you want, Vivi," Alison said.

Brady followed his sister inside, memories of the night he'd married Alison flooding him. The sky had been clear, the stars shining, the full moon silvery.

"How about simple white ribbons to rope off the seating area for the family?"

"Sounds great. Oh, and I want candles. Don't you think a candlelight service will be romantic, Brady?"

Brady rubbed a hand along the sleek wood of a pew as he walked toward the pulpit. "I'm sure Joe will love it."

Alison's gaze met his and he froze. She was standing in the same spot she'd stood in when they'd said their vows. He could see her taking his hand, gazing at him with love and adoration, whispering her promises, giggling when he'd kissed her twice instead of the traditional once.

God, he wanted to kiss her again.

"Brady, now you stand there. I need to see how the wedding party will look."

Vivica shoved him forward so he was standing in the groom's spot. Alison blushed and he stepped closer, mesmerized by the way she looked in the dim light seeping through the stained glass windows.

"It's a good thing I'm not having a dozen bridesmaids. This place is kind of small," Vivica commented.

"It's a great chapel," Brady said.

"I like small, intimate weddings, myself," Alison murmured.

"I'm going to check out the bride's room downstairs," Vivica whispered.

Brady heard her shoes tapping as she walked down the stairs.

Alison's dark eyes raked over the pulpit. "Her wedding's going to be lovely."

Brady nodded, but he wasn't thinking about his sister's wedding. He was remembering his own, and how little time he had left until his marriage ended. With that thought on his mind, he did what he'd wanted to do since he'd left Alison at the pool.

He reached out, pulled her into his arms and kissed her again.

Chapter Twelve

Alison melted into Brady's arms, so desperate for his kiss she felt as if she would have withered up and died if he hadn't finally succumbed. She'd wanted him when she'd felt his presence this morning at the pool, and, after that kiss, had fantasized about tossing her swimsuit aside, climbing out of the pool naked and having him follow her to the locker room and the shower....

Who was she kidding? She'd wanted him ever since she'd seen him standing on that parade float the first day he'd returned.

His lips tasted like fire, ravaging her with heat and hunger. She slid her hands to his chest, felt his heart pounding beneath her palms, felt his muscles tense as she stroked upward and dug her fingers into his hair. His hands dragged her closer, one tunneling through her own hair to draw her closer as his tongue probed the recesses of her mouth, licking, sucking, tasting, torturing.

They had said their vows right here in this chapel and had sealed their promises with a kiss. She felt that same yearning in his touch she'd felt years ago and realized that at least for now Brady still wanted her—no matter how much he kept pushing her away.

His lips blazed a trail across her cheek, then down her jaw and neck, and Alison moaned and pulled him closer. But footsteps tapped behind them, bringing her back to reality.

Brady tensed as if he heard them, too.

They slowly pulled apart. Alison tried to steady her breathing, hurriedly tucking her hair back in place. Brady shifted, stuffing his hands into his pockets.

"The bride's room is perfect," Vivica sang from the back of the church. "Anything else we need to talk about, Ali?"

Alison smiled shakily, grateful Vivica was at least acting as if she hadn't seen them. Of course, after Vivi's suggestion earlier—that Alison seduce Brady—she was probably silently cheering.

"No, I think everything's in good shape."

"Great."

Brady busied himself pretending interest in the woodwork. Alison decided to give him a moment to gather his composure, and went to the back of the church to meet Vivica. "Come on, let's check the outside, see where you want to set up the reception. You still want to have it outside if it's pretty, right?"

"Absolutely."

Alison grabbed Vivica's arm and guided her to the lake, desperately wondering what Brady was thinking.

BRADY STARED at the pulpit, the stained glass windows, the candelabra, and felt a peace he hadn't known in a long time.

Odd, since he'd just kissed the daylights out of Alison.

But standing in the spot where they'd promised each other their love, feeling her in his arms again, he almost felt whole again. He could almost forget about the accident. About Josh.

No, he thought, panic streaking through him. He could never forget about Josh and what had happened. He owed his friend that much loyalty.

The familiar anxiety pressed in on him, the nightmarish voices echoing in his head. He fisted his hands and walked outside to see if Vivica was ready to go home. Alison and his sister stood by the lake, laughing and planning where to set up the tables for the reception. A moment of regret attacked him: had things been different, he and Alison might be making plans for their future.

Plans for a home, children and a life together, not a divorce.

WHEN ALISON ARRIVED HOME, she removed the wedding photo from the hope chest and set it on her dresser. The imprint of Brady's lips on hers still burned. His hands on her body had turned the hunger into an ache of desire. He'd felt it, too—she knew he had, although when he'd exited the church, she'd seen that wall go up between them again.

She was going to break down that barrier and find out why Brady had decided they couldn't be together.

Determination filling her, she made some hot tea and settled on the chaise to reread some of his old letters.

Dear Alison,

I bet you thought I'd forgotten our anniversary, but I didn't—a year ago today we were married. I've had you on my mind all day. It's night now and I'm in my bunk, wishing I was there and we could celebrate together. When I lie down and close my eyes, I can see you standing in the soft candlelight of the chapel. I can hear your voice whispering my name, promising to be my wife, to love me for better or for worse.

I know it stinks that we're apart, and technically we're not still married, since your dad filed those papers, but in my head I'm still your husband. The guys here like to talk about all the women they…you know how guys talk, and I feel like a geek sometimes, because I don't care about having a bunch of women. All I want is you.

I hear the guys coming now and I better close this so they don't razz me to death. But I meant what I said, baby. You're the one in my dreams at night, and I'm always hot with wanting you. Sometimes it's just plain torture thinking about you, remembering that night we made love by the lake. But that memory keeps me going—until we can be together again.

Happy anniversary.
Love always,
Brady

Alison closed the letter and traced her finger over the picture frame, running her fingertip along the outline of Brady's face. In the photo, she'd been wearing her prom dress, summer flowers blooming in the background. If she married again, she wanted to have a traditional gown—and she knew the one she wanted. She'd seen it in the catalogue today. Feeling like a wistful child, she found the catalogue and cut out the picture. It was an original designer gown, with an off-the-shoulder lace bodice, and a matte satin scalloped skirt. She placed the photo inside her hope chest and smiled, thinking of Grammy Rose and the fact that she'd disagreed with her father about filing the papers. Maybe Grammy Rose had had some kind of premonition that Alison and Brady were meant to be together.

She glanced back at the picture and smiled. "I'm not giving up on you, Brady. Not yet."

"ALISON IS JUST SO wonderful," Vivica said as she climbed from the car. "She's smart and organized and has a great business mind. In high school did you ever think she'd turn out to be such a good businesswoman?"

"No, Vivica, I didn't." Brady gritted his teeth. The entire way home he'd heard nothing but praise for Alison.

"And you have to admit she's more beautiful now than she was then."

"Uh-huh."

"You know, I'd be surprised if she stays in Sugar Hill forever, though. Some guy is going to come

along, realize what a prize she is and sweep her out
of here.''

''That's enough, Vivi.''

Vivica turned a saccharine smile his way.
''Enough what?''

''Enough of a sales pitch on Alison.''

''What?'' Vivica lay a hand over her heart. ''I
was just making conversation, Brady.''

''Yeah, right.''

He headed toward the bedroom, anxious to get
away from her meddling, but his mother caught him
in the hall.

''There you are, son. Do you have a minute?''

''What for, Mother?''

''To talk about the print shop, of course.''

Brady frowned. ''No, Mom, not right now.''

She seemed shocked, but he ignored her reaction,
went into his bedroom and shut the door. Five
minutes later, he was sitting on his balcony, basking
in his privacy, with a Scotch and Alison's letters.

Dear Brady,
It's Thanksgiving here and the whole family
got together. Did I tell you Hannah's in med
school now? She's so smart, but we all knew
she'd be a success someday. On the flip side,
Mimi dropped out of school. Get this, she
wants to be an actress. I think she'd be really
great at it, but Dad had a cow. I haven't seen
him that upset since the night you and I got
married.

I got the letter you wrote on our anniversary
and I'm glad you remembered. I went out to

the lake that night and took a picnic, Brady. I know it sounds silly, but I pretended you were there and we were renewing our vows. I even snitched a bottle of wine from Dad's cupboard and had a sip, just to toast our special day.

The lake was so quiet and beautiful. I lay on the blanket and stared at the moon; it was a quarter moon hung low in the sky, and while I watched the thousands of stars twinkling down at me, I thought about you, Brady. About how I felt the first time I met you. The minute I saw you, my heart started pounding like a freight train—I knew you were going to be the one. The guy I'd saved myself for.

I'm closing my eyes now, Brady, pretending you're here with me, that you've snuck into my bedroom and it's oh so dark, and you crawled under the covers. Of course, I'm lying here waiting for you, naked and lonely and wanting to feel you touch and kiss me so bad I hurt. I think about your lips on mine, your tongue teasing my body, filling me, making me yours forever, and I'm so aroused I don't know if I can sleep. But if I do, Brady, I'll dream of you. And one day I know those dreams will come true, that you'll be here again, in my arms, in my bed, sharing my kisses and loving my body as a husband should.

> I love you forever & ever & always,
> Alison

Brady almost crushed the letter in his fist. Dammit, he wanted to do that, to love her body the way a husband should. To hold her and kiss her and drive her insane with his lips and his hands and his pulsing need.

He stared at the words again and picked up a pen. He hadn't written a letter in a long time. But after that heated kiss, he felt the urge to write Alison.

Dear Alison,
I don't even know where to begin. It's been so long since I've written you, since we've really talked, and there's so much to tell you. All about the long months I was away, about how I thought of you every day and wondered what you were doing, if you were still writing me, if you still dreamed of me at night.
   And there's the accident. I don't know if I can ever tell you about that. But it's changed me and I…

He paused, not knowing what to say. Frustrated, he suddenly balled up the paper and hurled it into the trash. What good would writing letters do now? Alison might still have feelings for him, but she loved the old Brady, the memories—the football star, the athlete, the fighter pilot.

And until he could fly again, he could never be that man.

THE NEXT MORNING Alison took her time stretching before she dove into the pool. She knew Brady would be there, that he would be watching. She'd seen him in the gym when she'd arrived. Apparently he'd decided to add a morning workout on the machines to his physical therapy sessions with Vivica.

Maybe he was getting back in shape so he could return to the Air Force.

The idea of him leaving before the month ended sent panic streaking through Alison. But if it meant Brady would be flying again, she'd have to let him go.

She moved easily into her routine, feeling the cool water infuse her with energy and calm her nerves. One stroke, then another... She glided through her laps, finally switching to the breaststroke, then onto her back to cool down.

She saw the barest hint of his shadow in the distance. Her breathing hitched in her throat but she tried not to react. She'd worn a skimpier bathing suit today, a one-piece cut so high on her thigh it almost veed to her waist. The midsection was cut out, the bodice connected to the bikini bottom by sheer lace, the low-cut top emphasizing her breasts. They were tingling now, not only from the cool water but from the heat of Brady's eyes.

She arched her back and rolled her shoulders, smiling when she saw Brady step through the doorway. Her whole body shivered with arousal, throwing her off her stroke. Then he retreated into the shadows again and her heart sank. Why had he come forward and kissed her yesterday, yet left her cold and alone today?

Just what was it going to take to get through to the man?

Chapter Thirteen

The next two and a half weeks dragged by. Alison was just about ready to pull her hair out and strangle Brady. Their relationship had stagnated just like the weather outside. He watched her swim every morning, yet he still hadn't left the shadows to join her. She and Brady and Vivica met frequently to finalize plans for the wedding, but he always managed to avoid being alone with her.

She wanted him more than ever.

But their divorce would be final in a week.

She glared at the phone, willing Vivica to see her expression. "Why can't *you* meet Brady for the tux fitting?"

"Because I have an extra physical therapy session to do and I forgot to tell Brady."

Alison tapped her foot on the floor. Vivica was definitely scheming. "I think Brady can manage by himself."

"Look, Ali, he's exhausted from his therapy session, and I'd feel much better if someone drove him."

"What about your mother?"

"She's up to her eyeballs in pink paper, making copies for that church charity event."

Alison rolled her eyes. "All right. But I'm not sure it's going to do any good—"

"What do you mean? Is something wrong with the tuxes?"

"Stop playing innocent, Vivi. I know you're matchmaking. And I've been doing my best for two weeks to be—"

"Seductive?"

"Available." Alison sighed. "But Brady doesn't seem to be interested."

"He's just so damn stubborn," Vivica said.

"Has he mentioned taking over the print shop lately?"

"No, I think we're making progress. I saw his flight manuals in his room yesterday." She hesitated another beat, then added, "So don't give up, Ali."

Alison began organizing her desk before she left. "You know, my ego is taking a real beating here."

Vivica chuckled. "Your ego will be fine, especially when Brady comes to his senses."

Alison said goodbye, hung up and grabbed her keys. Brady was going to be surprised when she showed up at the hospital to pick him up.

BRADY GUZZLED a bottle of water while he waited for Vivica to pick him up. The last thing he felt like doing was going to try on a tux, but he wanted to make his sister's wedding perfect for her. After all, as grueling as her therapy sessions were, he had to admit he was making progress, all due to Vivica's encouragement. His leg felt stronger every day, and adding the weight machines at the gym had rebuilt his upper body strength.

Of course, his libido was in worse shape than ever. Seeing Alison at the pool only made him want her more, but he'd have to live with that ache. Another week and he'd return for his evaluation. He'd probably be pushing desk duty for the next month. Then his enlistment time would be up and he'd have to decide what to do with his life.

A pink Cadillac drove up and he did a double take, then laughed. Wacky Wiley. He'd obviously driven Mimi to the hospital. The two of them got out, and Wiley helped Mimi climb the stairs.

"Hey, Brady," Mimi called.

"You're not here to deliver, are you?"

Mimi laughed. "No, I just came to meet Seth for our Lamaze class. Dad drove me so we wouldn't have two cars."

Wiley placed his hand on Mimi's back. "I told her she ought not to be driving this far along."

Mimi shook her head. "Men. If Dad and Seth had anything to do with it, they'd put me in a plastic bubble until this baby arrives."

Wiley looked haggard. "We can't help it if we're protective."

Mimi hugged her father. "I know, Dad, but relax and stop worrying. And thanks for the ride." She turned and waddled inside.

Brady stared after Mimi, suddenly envisioning his own wife pregnant. Alison. The two of them coming to the hospital. He'd be protective, too.

Wiley leaned against the post, his breathing ragged.

"Are you all right, Mr. Hartwell?"

Wiley dabbed at the perspiration with a lemon-yellow handkerchief. "I will be when that baby gets here. You can't imagine what it's like to worry about your kids."

Sadness gnawed at Brady. No, if he divorced Alison, he'd probably never have children. He couldn't see himself marrying another woman.

Wiley cleared his throat. "I'm glad I ran into you, son."

Brady looked at him in surprise. "Excuse me?"

"I've been wanting to talk to you, ever since that day at the parade."

Brady crunched the water bottle in his hand and tossed it in the garbage.

Wiley pointed to the steps and they both sat down. "I hear you've done well in the Air Force, earned your flying license."

"Yes, sir," Brady, said, feeling like a fake. "I'm a first lieutenant."

Wiley nodded. "Ali said you always wanted to fly. Glad to see you made something of yourself."

Brady dangled his hands over his knees, watching the cars pass, hoping Vivica would hurry up.

"I hope there aren't any hard feelings between us about that night," Wiley said.

He didn't have to say which night. Brady knew.

"I love my girls, you see. They're the only things that really matter to me." Wiley dusted a fleck of dirt from his paisley shirt. "I know I'm a loud old man and folks think I love that car dealership, but let me tell you, son, it's just a way to make a living.

Those girls, though, they're what my life's been all about. I gave up the service to be with them.''

Brady angled his head, his throat feeling slightly thick at the emotions he heard in Wiley's voice.

Wiley cleared his own throat. ''When I found out you and my baby girl married that night, I went off the deep end. But I thought I was doing the right thing, protecting Ali.'' He hesitated, his face flushing. ''She was getting ready to go to college and I knew I was going to lose her.''

Brady smiled. ''I think I understand. My dad gave up a career in the Air Force to be with us.''

''It's all worth it.'' A crooked smile curved Wiley's mouth, accentuating the age lines. ''I've often wondered if I was wrong about the annulment, though.''

Brady's head jerked up. ''Excuse me?''

''Yep. I still think Ali was too young to get hitched, but hell, what does love know about age? Sometimes you meet the right person when you're young, sometimes you might be ninety.'' He rubbed his chin, the whiskers bristling. ''I reckon what I'm saying is that if you and Ali pick up again, I won't stand in your way this time.''

''Uh…well, I appreciate that, but—''

Wiley stood with a grin. ''Hey, there's my baby now.''

Brady looked up in surprise as Alison parked in the front row of the parking lot, exited her car and walked toward them. She seemed surprised to see him talking to her father.

''Dad? Brady, what's going on?''

Wiley grabbed her in a bear hug. "Brady and I were just having a little man-to-man talk."

Alison frowned and wrapped her hands around her waist.

Brady stood. "I'd better go call Vivi. She's late."

"Brady, wait." Alison grabbed his hand. "Vivi's not coming. I'm driving you to the tux place."

Wiley pounded him on the back. "See you later, son. Nice talking to you." He tugged at the waist of his pants as he sauntered away.

Alison waved to her father, then turned to Brady, her eyebrow arched. "What in the world was that all about?"

ALISON STUDIED BRADY as they settled into her Jeep. "Brady, you didn't answer my question."

Brady fastened his seat belt, his expression tight. "I really could drive myself, you know."

"I know. But Vivica wanted me to personally check out the formal wear, and it's silly for both of us to drive. Now, what gives with you and my dad?"

Brady fiddled with the radio. "It was weird. He sort of apologized for that night."

Alison was so shocked she nearly drove over the curb. She quickly righted the car and glanced at Brady. "You're kidding, right?"

He shook his head. "Surprised me, too."

They lapsed into silence as she contemplated Wiley's change in attitude. "How's therapy going?" Alison finally asked.

He instinctively rubbed his injured leg. "Vivica's grueling, but it's getting better."

"What was the prognosis for recovery?"

His jaw tightened even more. "The doctor said I'll always have a slight limp. As far as being able to run a marathon, that's probably out."

"You never liked to run anyway, Brady. You preferred air travel."

A small smile curved his mouth, but sadness tinged his eyes. "Not being physically fit isn't conducive to a career in the Air Force, though. Not unless you want to push paper."

"You could still be a part of the military. If you stay here and run that print shop, you'll certainly be pushing papers."

Brady frowned but remained silent. Alison drove through the traffic, her shoulders tense. For such a virile man, being physically limited had to be terribly frustrating.

A few minutes later, they parked at the formal wear shop and Alison led the way inside. A tall, rail-thin salesman in his early thirties, dressed in a designer suit and funky glasses, helped her find the tux style Vivica and Joe had chosen.

"A great selection. The double layer lapel offers a sophisticated look. You like the notched collar?"

"Yes." Alison ran a thumb over the fabric. "Let's try the five-button coat."

"Yes, madame." He motioned to Brady. "We need to get your measurements, sir."

Alison watched as Brady stood at attention, his height topping the salesman's by a good six inches. Even in a chambray shirt, his broad shoulders looked amazingly wide, his arms fit and muscular. He stepped into the fitting room and Alison sucked in a deep breath when he emerged a few moments later. Tall, dark and handsome didn't begin to describe him. The black jacket accentuated his olive complexion and his jet-black hair.

She wanted him to take it off.

"I can't get this damn button fastened," Brady said, struggling with the neck of the shirt.

"Here, let me help." The salesman had disappeared, so Alison reached for the button, her hand brushing his shoulder. His muscles were so defined, his chest was like a hard wall. His masculine, earthy scent wafted toward her, making her dizzy. She had an insane urge to kiss him, to unbutton the shirt, toss it into the dressing room and show him how much she wanted him.

She felt his muscles tense as she touched his neck. "Relax," she whispered, unable to control the throaty, aroused sound. "I'm not going to choke you."

Brady chuckled, a deep rumble that sent a thousand delicious sensations skittering through her. "I'm not so sure. That bow tie looks pretty scary."

Alison laughed and slipped the button through its hole, her breath hitching as she stared at his neck, the bottom of his chin, that broad jaw with the hint of dark beard stubble visible in the overhead lights. Brady had been a young man when he'd left Sugar Hill, but he'd matured into an adult. She took the bow tie and began to fasten it, her hands trembling as he tensed even more.

He was so close his breath bathed her face and she could feel the heat emanating from his skin. Suddenly his hands covered hers, holding them to his chest. She felt the rapid beating of his heart, the warmth of his desire in his look, the evidence of his arousal against her thigh.

His big hand came toward her, one finger gently tracing her cheek. His eyes told her everything—how much he wanted her, all the things he wanted to do to her.

Alison couldn't resist any longer. She stood on tiptoe, pulled his face close to hers and whispered in his ear, "Brady, I want you." A tingle rippled up her spine when his labored breathing brushed her cheek. "Please, let's go somewhere and be together."

Chapter Fourteen

Brady gazed into Alison's eyes, ready to take her up on her whispered offer, but everything happened at once.

The salesman returned. Alison's cell phone rang. And the fire alarm sounded.

They both jerked apart to see the manager's beefy face turning red. "We're going to have to evacuate."

Alison answered her phone as she headed to the door. "Dad, hey, no, everything's okay." She paused. "Yes, it's a fire alarm. It's probably just a test, Dad. I'll call you back when we're outside."

Brady ducked into the dressing room and changed in sixty seconds. As soon as he emerged, he grabbed Alison's hand and they followed the crowd hastily exiting the mall. As they reached the car, a fire truck screeched up. The parking lot had fast become a scene of mass hysteria, and a thin stream of smoke billowed from a candle shop two doors down.

"Gosh, I hope no one is hurt," Alison said.

Brady nodded, then sighed in relief when a fire-man exited, announced they'd contained the blaze with no injuries, and explained the cause. Brady and Alison found the salesman who had assisted them standing beside a lamppost, shaking.

"Mr. Brentano?" Alison asked.

"Yes?" He smoothed down his suit, gathering his composure. "We have your measurements, sir. Just stop by in a couple of days, and we'll make sure everything fits."

Brady thanked him, and Alison handed him a business card. "Please call me to confirm when the groomsmen come in," she stated. "There are only a few days left before the wedding and we don't want any last-minute surprises."

The man agreed, and Brady and Alison headed to the car. "I'd better call Dad back right away," Alison said. "If I don't, he'll be here in a panic."

Before she could finish the sentence, Wiley barreled into the parking lot near them in a loaded Trans Am and jumped out, his lime-green jacket flapping about him.

"Are you okay, honey?"

"Yes, Dad, calm down. Everyone's fine."

"Where's the fire?"

"They've contained it. It turned out somebody lit a match in the candle store and things got out of hand."

Wiley gave her a once-over, then hugged her to him, and Alison laughed. "Dad, you worry too much."

Wiley reared back and ran a hand through his hair. "Listen here, you're my baby and I'll worry about you till you're old and gray." He finally noticed Brady and hesitated. "I'm glad you're here."

"Excuse me?" Brady jammed one hand into his pocket.

Wiley laid a hand on Brady's shoulder. "Listen, son, I had a pilot lined up to run this advertisement for me tomorrow, but he had a family emergency. I was wondering if you'd do me a favor and fly the ad for me."

Brady's stomach turned over. "Um, Mr. Hartwell, I—"

"I'll pay you good money, son. The local news is all set to cover it. All you have to do is fly low, waving this sign over the dealership—"

"I can't, Mr. Hartwell. I'm really sorry, but you'll have to find someone else."

Wiley argued with him, promising to double the salary, but Brady made up several excuses. When Wiley left, Brady's stomach clenched at the disappointment in Alison's eyes.

"Why won't you help Dad?" Alison asked.

Brady tensed. What could he say? He opened his mouth to offer her the same lame excuses he had her father, but he could see in her eyes that she hadn't believed him.

"Are you holding a grudge because of what he did to us four years ago?"

Brady shook his head. He couldn't let her believe he was so callous he'd harbor a grudge against her father. What kind of man would that make him?

"Brady, please talk to me." She laid a palm against his cheek. "A few minutes ago, I practically threw myself at you." Her voice broke. "The least you could do is be honest with me."

He felt like a heel.

He had hurt her once by cutting her out of his life without an explanation, and she was right. He owed her the truth. Once she knew how he'd let his friend down, she wouldn't want him anymore. Then she'd accept that their marriage was over, and move on.

He took her hand in his, and said in a low voice, "Okay, let's go to the lake. Then I'll tell you everything."

ALISON HAD NEVER SEEN Brady look so grave. She parked along the lake at the special spot where they used to come during high school. Nothing much had changed—oak and pine trees still shaded the lake, the scents of honeysuckle and wildflowers filled the air. The sun hung low, its orange light glinting off Brady's face as he settled on the ground. He picked up a rock and threw it, watched it sail across the lake and splash, then reached for another. Frogs croaked and crickets chirped around them. She could almost feel the tension in his body, the anger and confusion and pain radiating from him.

Alison studied the water and let the silence envelop them, hoping the peacefulness of the lake would seep into him, hoping the calm serenity would enable her to accept what he had to say.

He was going to tell her he didn't love her anymore and to stop throwing herself at him. She had to brace herself.

"I…I'm sorry I couldn't help your father."

"Couldn't or wouldn't?"

He glanced at her, then down at the rock, rolling it between his fingers. "Couldn't."

"I don't understand."

"It has to do with the accident." His breathing sounded harsh in the quiet. "I told you my best friend died in the crash."

"He was the guy from Missouri you wrote me about?" He nodded and Alison took a steadying breath, willing him to continue. It took him several seconds before he spoke again.

"Josh and I met my first year in flight school. He was a good guy, just wanted to make a better life for himself."

"He sounds a lot like you."

Brady nodded, his gaze fixed on the lake. But Alison sensed his mind was miles away.

"We were sent on a lot of training maneuvers, simulated combat battles."

"That was when you first stopped writing."

"Yeah." He tossed another rock in the water, and waited until it pinged and sank before he continued. "On the last training exercise, we were both getting cocky. We were the best in our flight unit. Josh had quick instincts, I had steady hands. We were flying fighter jets in a simulated combat situation, Josh decided to do some fancy stunts to show off." Brady closed his eyes, his voice husky. "But something went wrong. Josh got caught in the backwash from another plane, accelerated too quickly, lost control, and almost hit the side of the mountain. His belly clipped it, he lost a wing, then engine power. He thought he could land the jet but he couldn't make it. I told him to eject."

Alison twisted her hands in her lap, aching for Brady. She could see that he was tormented by the memories, had relived them a thousand times.

"But his eject button malfunctioned. He was yelling over the radio. I tried to talk him through it, but he panicked. The plane...it went down with Josh in it."

"Oh, Brady." She pulled his hand into hers. It felt limp, his fingers cold, as if the life had drained from him. And in a way, she realized, it had.

"I managed to pull up in time, barely avoided hitting a military building. By the time I landed and made it to his plane, it exploded."

"That's how you were hurt? You were trying to save him?"

Brady didn't respond. He'd lapsed into a world of his own. "I had to get him out of there. I had to save him."

Alison squeezed Brady's hand, imagining the horror of what he was describing.

"I saw Josh, the jet in flames, the smoke billowing everywhere." He pulled away from her, cradled his face in his hands, obviously trying to block the images. "I could smell the gas, the smoke, the burning jet. Then there was Josh's face, covered in blood. The fire was eating at him, licking up his clothes, singeing his hair." Brady's voice broke, but he continued, choking and crying now. "I tried to get to him, to pull him out, but the fire was too quick, and the plane kept burning."

Alison couldn't stand it anymore. She pulled him into her arms and cradled him against her, stroking his hair and rubbing his back while he wept.

"It was my fault, don't you see? If Josh and I hadn't tried to best each other, he might have tried to eject sooner."

"Oh, Brady…"

"I should have died, too, not just him. He was a good pilot…"

"Shh, I'm sure he was. Just like you are." His voice broke again, and Alison rocked Brady back and forth, tears trickling down her cheeks as she tried to soothe him. "It wasn't your fault, Brady, you can't blame yourself."

"But he shouldn't have died, and I received this damn hero's welcome here in Sugar Hill when I'm not a hero, Ali. I'm not."

Alison's heart broke for him. She cupped his face in her hands and forced him to look at her.

"Brady, your friend's death wasn't your fault. Accidents happen. You said yourself the eject button malfunctioned. You couldn't have known that would happen."

BRADY STARED into Alison's eyes, wanting to believe her, craving the redemption and forgiveness he heard in her voice. Craving the solace he felt in her arms. In her touch.

She must have sensed his vulnerability, because she lowered her head and brushed her lips across his, so loving, so tender, so sweet.

"I know you're hurting, Brady, and I want to help you." She traced a finger along his cheek, her voice a soft whisper. "I love you, Brady. I always have."

He closed his eyes, her tremulous words rolling over him, causing a bittersweet ache to swell in his chest. He suddenly couldn't stop himself. He was hurting, and Alison was the guiding light to relieve that ache. He wanted to love her, to give her pleasure. Wanted it so badly he thought he'd explode.

He threaded his fingers into her hair, dragged her face to his and kissed her. Her lips tasted like the finest of wines, sweet and delicious. He sipped at her mouth, ran his tongue across it, then delved inside to take as much as she offered. She returned his hunger with a moan of acquiescence, fueling his passion even more when she savagely clawed at his shirt. Buttons popped and flew across the grass. He tossed the shirt to the ground and groaned when she lowered her head and dropped kisses along his jaw, down his neck, then took his hard nipple in her mouth and teased it with her tongue. It had been four years, four damn miserable years without her.

He pulled at her blouse, found the bottom and tugged it over her head, then paused to drink in the sight of her. She wore a lacy, pale pink bra, her firm breasts spilling over the edges. His body hardened to a painful ache, pulsing against her thigh, and he lowered his head and nibbled at her flesh. She moaned and arched her back, thrusting herself into him, and he unfastened her bra, flung it to the ground and began to suckle her—first one breast, then the other, greedily taking pleasure as she writhed against him. Her legs intertwined with his, her moans music to his ears.

His only thought was to give her pleasure. To love her and show her all the ways he'd wanted her the past four years.

He cupped her hips, dragged her skirt down inch by inch and trailed kisses along her stomach, down her thighs. Then he pushed her skirt to her ankles, taking her panties with it.

"Brady—"

"Shh, honey, let me love you." He nibbled at her knees, at her inner thighs, at the secrets she had held for him all these years. Her body was so voluptuous, her long slender legs stretched out beneath him, her womanhood bared for his eyes to feast upon. "Do you know how many times I've dreamed of doing this the past four years?"

She raked her fingers through his hair. "I've dreamed of it, too."

"I've wanted you every night…" he flicked a tongue against her heat "…naked and moaning and…" he thrust his tongue inside, suckled her "…with your legs open for me, your voice calling my name as I make you cry with ecstasy."

She clawed at his back. "Oh, Brady, I love you…"

Her voice broke off as he buried his face in her heat and tormented her until he tasted heaven. She pulled at his arms, tried to move him up to join their bodies, but he savored her honeyed taste, refusing her. This time was for her, only her, so he held her still and took pleasure in the sensation of the shivers racking her body. Finally, her moans grew quieter, her voice a whimper.

"Brady, please, I want you to hold me."

He slowly rose above her, looked into her eyes, saw the heat and passion and love, and his heart ached even more. If only he had more to give her.

Birds twittered in the background; a duck

splashed. Somewhere a car backfired, the sound reminding him of the explosion.

She reached for his belt buckle. He caught her hand, brought it to his fingertips, kissed each finger, then shook his head.

"But I want to love you, Brady. Why won't you let me?"

Her heart was in her eyes, and he silently cursed himself for hurting her again. He stood, grabbed his shirt, yanked it on and turned to the lake, trying to calm his raging emotions.

ALISON HAD NEVER FELT such sweet, hot ecstasy in her life.

Yet she'd also never felt so alone as when Brady loved her, then pushed her away.

Her hands trembling, she gathered her clothes, slipped them back on, then grabbed his arm, trying to force him to face her. "I asked you why you're pushing me away, Brady, and I want an answer."

He hated the quiver in her voice, hated even more that he still had demons to face, that he couldn't be what she wanted. "Because nothing's changed."

Anger balled in Alison's stomach. "That's not true, Brady. We established two things here today."

He swung around and glared at her. "What? That we both wanted sex."

Hurt stabbed through her. "That we both wanted *each other*." She firmed her chin. "If you'd wanted sex, you could have had that with anyone the past four years. But you admitted you haven't been with anyone, Brady."

His gaze cut back to the lake, his own jaw set.

"And now I understand why you're pushing me away. You feel guilty over your friend's death."

"I am guilty," he said harshly. "I have the scars inside and outside to prove it." He gestured toward his jeans. "If we'd finished what we'd started, you'd see how ugly I am now, Alison. I'm not the high school football star you fell in love with, or the pilot."

"Is that why you think I fell in love with you? Because you were a football star?"

He averted his gaze, stared at his boots, crushed the dirt below them. "Isn't it, Alison?"

"No. I can't believe you think I'm that shallow." She folded her arms around her waist, furious. "I fell in love with you because you're you."

"But I'm not that same guy, Alison."

"Maybe not. But maybe you are. Maybe you're just a grown-up version."

"Growing up changes us, Ali."

"You had an accident, Brady, and so did your friend. It *was* an accident. It wasn't your fault. You have to forgive yourself, go back up and fly again."

Brady shook his head, his voice gruff. "That's just it. Don't you get it?" He swung around and held out his hands. They were shaking and his voice was filled with anguish. "I can't fly anymore, Ali. It's not that I didn't want to help your father, but I can't."

Alison reached out to touch him but he pulled away. "Why not, Brady? Because of your injuries? Did the doctors order you not to?"

"No," he said in a hoarse voice. "Because I'm too damn afraid."

Chapter Fifteen

Brady felt Alison's hand on his shoulder and tensed. He'd finally admitted the truth about himself, so why wasn't she turning away?

"Have you talked to someone about it, Brady?"

A sardonic chuckle escaped him. "What? You mean like a shrink?"

"It wouldn't hurt. Seth, Mimi's husband, is a psychiatrist and he's really nice—"

He shook his head. "No."

"Well, you told me. That's a start." She moved behind him and massaged his shoulders, kneading the knot at the base of his neck. "You should talk about how you feel, though, with Vivi or your mom or me. It's not good to hold your emotions inside you."

"Talking won't bring Josh back, Ali." He pulled away and headed to the car. "I think we'd better go."

"I'm not giving up on you, Brady Broussard," Alison called after him. "And you'd better not give up, either."

WHEN ALISON ARRIVED HOME, she was so tense she couldn't sleep. One moment she convinced herself she and Brady would work things out; the next she sensed a feeling of hopelessness and defeat in Brady she'd never imagined seeing.

Maybe time would turn his attitude around.

Except time was running out—their divorce would be final in a few days. She had a feeling if she didn't reach him before then, she'd lose him forever.

She skimmed through some of Brady's letters until she found one of the last ones he'd written her.

Dear Alison,

I'm starting my third year now and you've heard me talk about my friend Josh, the guy from Missouri. We have this competition thing going between us—you know how guys are. He played quarterback in high school, too, so we horse around with the ball on the weekends. And we're always trying to best each other in flight training. Maybe if I get some leave time soon, he can come home and meet you.

Then again, it's been so long since I've seen you, I want you just to myself. Lately, I've been thinking more and more about you. I hope you're liking school. (Not too much, though, at least not any of the guys.)

Sometimes I worry you'll fall for some other man, and I don't think I could stand it.

Every night I close my eyes and I see you standing at our spot down by the lake. Your sweet face is smiling at me, and I hear you whispering my name when I pull you into my arms. I can't wait to run my hands through your long dark hair (you didn't cut it, did you?) 'cause it felt like silk, and your naked body felt like heaven.

I wonder if you still remember what it felt like to kiss me, to have me touch you all over, to have me deep inside you. I can't wait to refresh your memory. God, I get hard just thinking about making love to you, Ali.

I'm going to put in for leave soon. I have to see you, even if it's just for a short weekend.

Love always,
your Brady

THE NEXT DAY Brady rose feeling slightly optimistic. Instead of the nightmare, he'd dreamed he was lying on a blanket beside the lake making love to Alison, her legs twined around him, her eyes staring into his, his body pumping into hers. They'd whispered promises of love and forever, and had even talked of having a family together.

He inhaled the fresh morning air as he stepped onto the balcony, settled himself in a patio chair with his coffee and his old flight manuals. His leg wasn't hurting as much, and although he physically still ached from wanting Alison, he felt a sense of euphoria from almost making love to her. At least he had given her pleasure.

Maybe he'd get over this post-traumatic stress syndrome and be able to fly again. Then he'd be the man Alison deserved.

Grateful his mother had left for an early breakfast with her church women's group, he studied the flight manuals, and decided to call Frost and set up a time to let him take him up in one of the Cessnas. It was a baby step toward flying, but Brady didn't trust himself to take the plane up by himself.

Still, it was a start.

Alison believed in him. She'd said she wasn't giving up on him; maybe he shouldn't give up yet, either.

He gathered the books and put them in his room, pausing when he saw the invitation he'd misprinted with his and Alison's names on it. Smiling to himself, he stuffed it in one of his manuals, then set out for his morning walk, heading toward the gym.

When he entered the pool area, Alison was finishing her laps. He inhaled the scent of chlorine and told himself he should have gone to the weight room first, but he hadn't been able to stop himself. He had to see her again.

She stopped swimming, turned on her back and floated to the side, then leaned against the edge, propped her arms on the tile and smiled at him as if she'd known he would come. Water glistened off her dark eyelashes and beaded her skin, giving it a translucent glow. Her white bathing suit dipped precariously low, hinting at the cleavage beneath and the womanly curves that filled it out.

She crooked a finger and whispered, ''I've been waiting for you.''

Unable to control himself, he walked toward her. His dream the night before echoed in his mind, and hunger exploded in his veins. She looked breathtaking, her nipples beading beneath the thin suit, her lips so rosy and kissable he had to taste her.

He knelt at the water's edge, reached out and cupped her chin in his hand and lowered his head. She arched her back and rose to meet him, her lips like wine to his thirst. He drank and sipped while she threaded her fingers in his hair.

"Why don't you come in?" she finally whispered when he broke the kiss to tease her ear with his tongue.

For once, he couldn't deny her. He'd been standing in the doorway watching her swim for weeks, each time aching to get in the water with her, to hold her and feel her come apart in his arms. He'd be leaving soon. He wanted the memory to take with him. And the place was deserted, as usual.

In one quick movement, he shrugged off his shoes and socks, tossed his shirt on a nearby chair and climbed in the water. Her gaze fastened on his chest, and he squared his shoulders, feeling heady and masculine and so in love he thought he might burst.

Brady felt staggered by that sudden realization. He did still love her, he silently admitted—no matter how much he'd tried to forget her, how many times he'd told himself he didn't deserve her. He couldn't deny his feelings any longer—at least not to himself.

She reached up and traced a finger along his collarbone, down his shoulder, around his nipple and he sucked in a sharp breath, wanting to take her right there in the water. A slow smile curved her lips and he grabbed her hands.

"You have a little bit of devil in your eyes this morning," he murmured.

"Maybe there's some unfinished business I've been thinking about."

Her soft, sultry voice only fueled his pounding heartbeat. He dragged her to him and slid his arms around her, cupping her buttocks and pulling her against him as he lowered his mouth over hers.

A loud cough reverberated behind him and he stiffened, silently waiting while Alison dropped her head against his chest and giggled.

"I gather we're not alone anymore," he said gruffly.

She nodded. "It's the senior citizens aerobics class. That's one reason I come so early to swim, so I can be out before they start."

Brady chuckled. "Guess I'd better go take a cold shower."

She brought his hand to her mouth and kissed his fingertips. "We'll finish this later, Brady. That's a promise."

"ONLY FOUR MORE DAYS and I'll be Mrs. Joe Rucker," Vivica exclaimed. "I'm so excited, Ali."

Alison smiled, secretly hoping in that four days she and Brady would work things out between them and she would still be Mrs. Brady Broussard. "I'm so happy for you, Vivi."

"Is there anything I need to do?"

Alison went down the checklist. "Videographer, taken care of. Catering set. Flowers on order. Hannah's agreed to keep the bride's book at the reception. The photographer will meet you there to take prewedding photos at five."

"What about your bridesmaid dress?"

"I tried it on this morning. It fits perfectly."

Vivica sighed. "And the musician?"

"Claire Follet is playing the piano." Alison looked up from the list. "How about the license and the wedding rings? Have you and Joe taken care of those?"

Vivica nodded. "Yep, got the license. And we picked out this gorgeous set of his-and-her matching bands. They're gold with a tiny hint of black etching."

"Sounds perfect, Vivi."

"I just hope the weather holds out," Vivica said. "I'd hate to have to move the reception inside."

"It's supposed to be clear," Alison said, although everyone in town knew they desperately needed rain. "But I've already checked out the reception hall downstairs and have extra decorations on hand in case we need them."

"Thanks, Ali, you've been a godsend."

Alison tapped her pen on the list. "Is Reverend Barnes going to perform the service?"

"Yes. He actually christened me and Brady."

Alison smiled at the image. Would he christen her and Brady's baby someday?

"Speaking of my brother, how are things going?"

Alison shrugged. "A little better, I guess."

Vivica squealed. "I just knew it. This morning I dropped by the house looking for Brady and I saw his old flight manuals on the desk. I accidentally knocked one off and this fell out." She lay a white wedding invitation on the table.

Alison gasped as she read the wording.

> Mrs. Inez Broussard requests the honor
> of your presence
> at the wedding of her
> son, Brady Broussard,
> to
> Alison Leigh Hartwell.

Her heart raced. Brady had written up an invitation as if they were getting married?

Then she read the time and date and realized it was the same time as Vivica's wedding. "I don't understand."

"I didn't, either, not at first," Vivica said. "Brady must be planning to surprise you. Maybe he wants you two to renew your vows at the church with us."

"But he wouldn't want to impose on your day. And he'd ask you first."

"Like I would care!" Vivica hugged her. "Brady knows I adore you and I want the two of you to stay together. Maybe he figures it'll be a good wedding present for me."

Alison's finger trembled as she traced the wording. Could it be true—could Brady be coming around? Could he be planning to ask her to renew their vows instead of finalize the divorce?

BRADY STEPPED FROM the shower, dried off, pulled on jeans and a polo shirt, then towel-dried his hair. His short military cut had grown slightly in the last month. He'd have to get it trimmed. He could hardly believe the month was almost over, that he'd be leaving Sugar Hill again.

And Alison.

All day he'd felt euphoric from their interlude in the pool. He'd thought about it while he'd worked at the print shop, during his session with Vivica, then afterward when he'd phoned George Frost and set up a time to go by the airport. George was going to take him up first thing in the morning. Brady grabbed the flight manual, stunned when he realized the invitation was missing. Before he could search for it, the doorbell rang and he heard his mother answer it. He was surprised to hear Alison's voice, then his mother's.

"Well, hello there, Alison. How's everything going?"

"Fine, Mrs. Broussard. You can relax, everything's set for the wedding."

Disappointment mushroomed in his stomach. So, she'd come by to discuss wedding plans, not to see him.

"Is Brady here?"

He jerked his head toward the door. She did want to see him!

"Yes, I'll go get him."

"I'm right here, Mom." Brady walked into the den, buttoning the last button on his shirt. "Hi, Alison."

A beatific smile warmed her face. "Hi."

His mother glanced from Alison to him, confusion wrinkling her brow.

"Did you need to talk to me about the wedding plans?" he asked.

"Oh, yes," Alison said, mischief lighting her

eyes. "We need to go for a final fitting for your tux."

He nodded and kissed his mother's cheek. "I'll be back later."

"Shall I hold dinner?"

"Actually, I thought Brady and I might grab something while we're out," Alison said. "That is, if you don't mind."

"Of course not, you kids enjoy yourselves. I'm going to work on Vivica's wedding gift. I'm cross-stitching a sampler with her wedding date on it."

"That sounds lovely," Alison said.

Brady gestured toward the door and they walked outside. The weather was hot and dry, as it had been most of the summer, the barest hint of a breeze bringing the scent of his mother's roses from the porch trellis.

"Are we really going for a tux fitting?" Brady asked as he climbed into Alison's Jeep.

Alison took him by the collar and pulled him toward her, then kissed him soundly. "No, I'm kid-napping you for the night, and we're going to finish what we started this morning."

ALISON HAD THOUGHT OF nothing all day but being in Brady's arms. After seeing that wedding invitation, she'd found her hopes for their future escalating hourly. She wanted to tell him she knew his secret, that she'd seen the invitation, but she bit back the words, not wanting to spoil the surprise.

In four days they would renew their vows.

Tonight, they would renew their passion.

And even if Brady didn't come around right after

they made love, their joining might give her more time, especially if what Vivica had told her about the technicality during the waiting period was true. Vivica wasn't sure, but she thought if they slept together, the thirty days started over.

Tingling with heady thoughts, Alison put in a Sting CD, one she knew was Brady's favorite, and drove toward the lake. With the sides to the Wrangler removed, the wind blew her hair around her face, teasing her with Brady's masculine scent as well.

He reached out and tucked a strand of hair behind her ear. "You look beautiful tonight, Ali."

It's because I'm so happy. "You look pretty handsome yourself."

He smiled—a real smile, for the first time since he'd returned. The sight did strange things to her insides and made her foot heavy on the gas pedal. Within minutes, they'd spread a blanket in a secluded area by the lake in the heart of a thicket of trees. They lay on the blanket and talked while dusk settled and darkness descended upon them. The moon spilled light on the grass and water, dappling rays across Brady's face, reminding her of all the times they'd been here together.

She set out a picnic of wine, shrimp salad, steak kabobs, and doughnuts for dessert.

"Doughnuts?" Brady held up the paper bag filled with chocolate éclairs, crème-filled doughnuts and coffee.

"I was thinking about our wedding night. We had doughnuts that night instead of cake, remember?"

He nodded, emotions shining in his eyes. "Of course, I remember."

She lit a candle. "And this is for all those candles I lit when I said a prayer for you."

His gaze turned more intense, his expression a mixture of hunger and dark passion. They ate and sipped wine as they stretched out on the blanket and stared at the stars.

Brady took her hand in his, threading their fingers together and cradling them against his chest. "Ali, you know I can't make any promises right now."

She bit down on her lip, his breathing raspy in her ears.

"I still have some big decisions to make about my career."

As long as he made them with her.

She rolled to her side and propped her head on her hand, gazing up at him. His color had returned and he'd gained a little weight since he'd been home. Some of the hollowness had dissipated from his eyes, as well.

She traced a finger down his jaw. "I have faith in you, Brady. I always have."

Her quietly spoken promise of trust seemed to touch him.

"It's not easy, when I think about Josh…"

"Shh." She pressed her finger to his lips. "If Josh loved flying as much as you and you shared this competitive spirit, then he wouldn't want you to give up."

Brady pressed his lips together and nodded.

"He'd want you to live, Brady, to have everything you've always wanted.'' She reached out and traced his lips with her finger.

He bit down on her fingertip, then pulled it into his mouth and suckled it.

She wanted nothing tonight except to take away all the pain he'd felt the last few months. To give him pleasure. So she pressed her mouth against his, drove her tongue inside, and began to undress him.

Chapter Sixteen

Brady had wondered if making love with Alison would be as wonderful as he'd remembered.

It was even better.

She tore at his clothes, plundered his mouth with her tongue, raked kisses along his naked chest and yanked off his pants and underwear. He didn't have time to worry about his scars, because she lowered her head and kissed his battered thigh before he could stop her.

"Alison, God, you don't have to do that."

She didn't listen.

She gently kissed the length of his thigh, massaged his calf, sat up astride him and tossed her flimsy red blouse to the blanket. "I can't believe you thought I'd care."

Like a fool, he found tears suddenly filling his eyes. All those months of being separated haunted him, of lying in the hospital, thinking she'd never want him again, that he'd lost her forever. Embarrassed, he bit the inside of his cheek and turned his head away. But Alison leaned over, framed his face with her hands and forced him to look at her. Then she brushed a tender kiss along his eyelids, and the emotions clogged his throat.

"I love you, Brady. I always have and I always will. For better or worse."

Before he could reply, she moistened her lips with her tongue and raised an eyebrow, giving him a mischievous look that forced him to smile. With a flick of her thumb, she dropped her bra beside her blouse, baring herself for his eyes to feast upon. And feast he did. His gaze lingered on the perfect curve of her breasts, on the dark pointed nubs, which he had to touch. He rolled each peak between his thumb and forefinger, smiling when she moaned and threw back her head, her long hair shimmering along her shoulders.

As an eighteen-year-old lover, she'd been giving and tender and incredibly sweet. As a woman she was entrancing and passionate and very erotic. He buried his face in her midriff, kissing and bathing her bare skin with his tongue, his hands skimming a path over her body, teasing her and finding her secrets. She rubbed herself against him, bringing him to a fevered pitch of arousal as her legs stroked his calves. With a rasp of pleasure, she lowered her head, letting her dark hair fall down to brush his chest, and drove her mouth downward again. His body sizzled with desire and hunger as she kissed the insides of his thighs, and finally, after long moments of torture, found his sex.

He threaded his fingers in her hair, closed his eyes and groaned, the intensity of his pleasure beyond anything he'd ever felt. Her hands slipped up to grab his, to hold him in her prison of torment as she brought him to the brink. And just before he thought he would explode with ecstasy, she rose up, shimmied out of her panties and angled herself so he could see their bodies as they joined. Brady's heart pounded as she lowered herself on him, gliding along his body and moving so seductively he growled her name. Then she shoved his hands above his head, increasing the tempo of their rhythm, making him beg for her to let him touch her. She finally released his hands, and he instantly cradled her breasts, brought his lips to her hardened peaks and suckled her. She writhed and called out his name, clutching at his chest and crying out with her release. His heart squeezed at the beautiful sound, then their gazes locked, and love and passion darkened her eyes as he buried himself deep inside her and sailed home.

ALISON CURLED into Brady's arms, savoring every moment. His labored breathing mingled with the sounds of birds twittering in the trees, at crickets chirping. He hugged her to him, his big arm draped possessively around her shoulders. His other hand traced slow, lazy circles on her back, occasionally dipping lower to the indentation of her spine and waist. Should she tell him that, for her, anyway, this changed things about the divorce? Or would he think she'd tricked him?

"I wish we could stay like this forever," she whispered.

His chuckle rumbled near her ear. "So do I." Then he pulled her gently back, cupped her face with his hands and kissed her again. This time the kiss was so tender and full of emotion that Alison knew their love would last forever.

THE NEXT MORNING Brady sat up in bed, flexing his injured leg, the memory of Alison's sweet body pumping adrenaline through him. Last night had been real, not a dream or fantasy—he'd loved her over and over again, had memorized each contour of her body, each little sound she'd made when he'd brought her to ecstasy.

Alison believed in him.

Dammit, he was trying to believe in himself again. He owed her that much. He had to fight for himself and for her.

Brady gathered his courage, showered and wolfed down a muffin, then drove to the small airport outside town, determined to face his demons. George Frost was already there, preparing the Cessna. "You sure you don't want to take her up by yourself?" George asked.

Brady shook his head. "No, I should wait until I get clearance from my doctor. But I'd like to take a ride, if you've got the time."

"Sure, I can show you the county needing medical flight services."

"Great." Brady's heart was pounding so hard he thought he might have a heart attack. He buckled up, put on his headset and listened as George checked the weather report.

George scanned the checklist, making sure the plane was set to run. Plenty of fuel. Engine checked out. Controls working.

Brady took several deep breaths, trying to relax,

mentally going through the routine with George. The engine coughed and sputtered to life as the plane moved down the taxiway to the runway, then built up speed. Brady's pulse hammered, the familiar exhilaration of taking off seeping into him, the trees and landscape growing smaller as they lifted off and began to climb. Along with the adrenaline rush, waves of fear riddled him as they soared above the town. He realized he was holding his breath, and exhaled, praying he wouldn't have a panic attack.

But as the mountains shifted into view and George pointed out the isolated areas that needed medical services, Brady's fears escalated. He could picture Josh trying to avoid the mountain, pulling up, the plane crashing, fire exploding into the sky. The ambulance…

"There's Sugar Hill General," George was saying, "but of course, for severe cases—burn victims, etcetera—we'd transfer patients to one of the larger, better-equipped facilities in Atlanta."

Sweat beaded on Brady's face and trickled down his chin. Had he actually considered not reenlisting, and running the medical flight service?

How in the hell could he do that when flying made him break out in a cold sweat? The sight of an ambulance or another burn victim might send him over the edge. If he panicked midflight or at the sight of an injured patient, the results could be catastrophic. Defeat settled on his shoulders.

He couldn't live with anyone else's death on his conscience.

"I'M TELLING YOU, Vivi, he feels guilty about the accident and he's punishing himself," Alison said the next day, after they'd discussed the checklist for the wedding. She hated to disclose something Brady had told her in confidence, but felt Vivica should know the extent of his guilt. "It's affecting his ability to fly."

"I figured as much." Vivica checked the thank-you cards Alison had had preprinted for after the ceremony. "I'm glad he opened up to you, Ali. That's a good sign."

So was the fact that he'd made love to her. But they still hadn't discussed the divorce.

"I'll try to encourage him to talk to me about flying during therapy this afternoon."

"Please don't tell him I spoke with you about this. I don't want him to feel like I betrayed his trust." Alison closed the planning book, making a mental note to check with Mimi about the catering status. With only three days until the wedding, she wanted to make sure all the details were ironed out. "But I'm worried about him, Vivi."

"Don't worry, I won't even hint that we've talked." Vivica grabbed the lingerie she'd bought for her honeymoon.

"Did you get some racy stuff?" Alison asked.

Vivica nodded. "Joe's going to be shocked." She yanked out a pair of silver fishnet hose and a black teddy, along with his-and-hers fire-engine-red thongs.

"Wow. Where are you going on your honeymoon?"

"I don't know," Vivica said. "Joe said it's a surprise, but to pack light.'' She waved the undies. ''So I'm ready.''

Alison laughed. ''How romantic. Where is he, anyway? I thought he was coming back to town today.''

Vivica frowned. ''Me, too, but he's still trying to tie up that project.'' She checked her watch. ''Uh-oh, gotta go. My patients are waiting.''

''Don't forget we're giving you a bridal shower tomorrow evening.''

''Followed by a wild bachelorette party, I hope,'' Vivica said with a laugh.

''Of course.'' Alison waved goodbye, her gaze resting on the brochures the travel agent had left in the shop. The Caribbean? Rome? Paris? Hawaii?

They all sounded romantic. It was ironic that she still had a husband after four years, and for at least three more days, but she'd never had a honeymoon. Feeling wistful, she crammed the brochures in her purse. Maybe she'd put those in her hope chest. And if she and Brady renewed their vows after Vivica's wedding, she'd give him some ideas on where to go for their long-overdue getaway.

''SON, DO YOU HAVE a minute?''

Brady glanced up from the pamphlet he'd been working on and nodded. Might as well get this talk with his mother over with; he'd been stalling for days.

His mother set a cup of coffee in front of him before he could even ask for it. ''I missed you at breakfast.''

Brady sipped the hot coffee. "I had some things I wanted to do early."

"Were you at the gym again?"

"No, I went out to the airport on Route 9."

"What were you doing out there?"

Brady frowned at her question, noticing for the first time since he'd been home how much she'd aged. And how lonely she seemed, almost desperate for someone to talk to. She should get out more. "Hannah Hartwell mentioned Sugar Hill needing a medical flight service, and asked me to talk to the manager of the flight service about it."

"Oh." A nervous expression flitted across his mother's face.

"What's wrong, Mom?"

"Nothing, dear. I just wondered what you'd decided about coming back here to run the shop."

As if he'd thought about anything else last night except Alison.

After this morning, Brady didn't know why he wasn't committing to his mother. He'd certainly proven he wasn't capable of flying again. But he just couldn't run the shop.

"I don't think so, Mom. You know I have to return to duty for another month. I'm thinking of teaching classes."

Disappointment filled her eyes, but she brightened quickly. "All right, then Mr. Fairbank from church is going to help me at the shop for a while."

"That's good, Mom."

His mother placed a hand on his shoulder. "You won't be doing anything dangerous when you go back, will you?"

"No, Mom, I'll be pushing paper for a while. Why?"

Her chin quivered. "'Cause I couldn't stand to lose you. I already lost your father, and you're so much like him, honey, and…" Her voice trailed off, tears overflowing.

Brady stood, cleared his throat and pulled her into his arms. His mother was lonely, he realized, and still grieving over his father. At last Brady understood why his father had left military service. He'd given part of his life to the Air Force and decided to devote the other part to his family. "Shh, Mom, it's okay. I'm here and I'm fine now."

She lifted a hand and touched his cheek. "I know I'm a foolish old woman, but I've enjoyed having you here, Brady. Your dad would be so proud of you."

Brady's throat closed. If his father was alive and knew what had happened with Josh, would he be proud? Would he want Brady to stay here and take over the family business or go back to face his fear?

LATER THAT DAY after therapy, Brady was so exhausted he took a nap. Once again his sleep turned to nightmares.

He'd taken lessons to fly a chopper, and was flying the medical flight helicopter. He had tried to land in a remote part of the mountains to rescue some stranded hikers, when another call came in.

"Urgent! Three children and their mother are trapped in a burning house on Fleet Road."

He stared out the window. He could see smoke billowing through a thicket of trees. Flames shot from the old wooden cabin, quickly eating it like dry brush. He had to take the chopper down, had to hurry.

He tried to land, but his vision blurred. Panic seized him. The controls slipped from his hands. The chopper spun out of control. Someone on the radio yelled his name.

He jerked back to reality, took the controls, whipped the chopper over the trees, dove down to land in the clearing. Hurry, hurry, you have to save them. *He ran, panting and heaving. Josh's bloody face appeared in the woods, and Brady shook his head to clear his vision. The kids, the woman, they needed saving. He ran on, limping and pushing at the brush. Fire shot toward the sky. The scent of smoke filled the air. Heat radiated from the burning cabin, scorching his face. His ears were ringing, Josh's cry for help bleeding into the present. Another shrill scream pierced the air—a child's scream echoing through the canyon.*

He froze. He'd never reach them in time. The roof of the cabin crashed in, wood hissed; the fire singed his arms as he reached through the broken window. The inside was ablaze, engulfed in fire. He couldn't save them....

He woke with a start and jerked upright, drenched in sweat, his heart pounding. Balling his hands into fists, he stood and paced across the room, opened the balcony doors and inhaled the balmy August air, trying to block out the images. Sweat poured off his face; his body was shaking, his pulse hammering. Gripping the door, he steadied himself, fighting off the images, the horrible cries, the fire and death.

Across the street, a light still burned in the upper bedroom of Alison's apartment. He ached for her, wanted her to hold him and make all the nightmares disappear.

But he couldn't ask that of her. She'd already given him so much. But she wanted, she *expected* him to resume flying. And he had tried this morning.

But he didn't have it in him. And he wouldn't let her settle for less than she deserved.

Exhausted, he stumbled toward the corner desk, pulled out a piece of paper and a pen and began to write.

Dear Alison,
Next to watching Josh die, writing you tonight is the hardest thing I've ever done. Leaving you next week will even be harder. But I have to go after Vivi's wedding. I have another month of my enlistment time left, and will be pulling desk duty until my evaluation is complete. I'm not sure what I'll do then, but I know now I won't be able to fly again, not in the Air Force, not here in Sugar Hill.

Yes, if you're wondering, I did try. I went out to the airport and rode up with George Frost, but I kept seeing the crash and Josh's face. The Air Force doctor said I had post-traumatic stress syndrome. I guess he was right. But it means I'm pretty useless in a plane or an emergency. I hope Hannah finds someone qualified to fly the medical flight service chopper, but it can't be me. I still want to use my skills somehow. I told Mom I'm not going to run the print shop. I may reenlist and try desk duty or teach some classes.

All I know is that we can't be together. You are the most wonderful woman I've ever known, but I can't ask you to settle for a man who's not whole. Alison, please know I've loved you every minute of my life and will always treasure the time we were together. Especially last night. Making love to you again was something I've fantasized about for years, and I'll keep that memory with me forever.

When I leave, I'll dream of you in my bed and in my arms, but always the way it used to be between us. That's the way I want you to remember me, too—the way I used to be, strong and tough, a man of adventure. Your high school football star, your Air Force pilot, your hero.

Love always,
your once-husband, Brady

Chapter Seventeen

Alison breezed across the pool, grateful for the calming lull of the water. Although she'd fallen asleep sated and euphoric, more optimistic than she had been since Brady returned, she'd woken up at dawn with a bad premonition.

Switching into the breaststroke, she inhaled, pushed her feet into the stroke and settled into a comfortable pace. Suddenly she sensed that Brady was watching.

Surely after last night he didn't intend to linger in the shadows.

Maybe he wanted a repeat of yesterday.

She crossed the pool twice more, then turned on her back, swam to the side and arched her arms over the edge of the pool, searching for him.

He stepped from the doorway, his masculine presence almost overpowering. He was wearing a blue T-shirt that stretched across his muscular chest like a glove, and black running shorts that accentuated his height. Dark hair covered his arms and legs, the jagged scar running from his calf around his battered knee up into his shorts.

Even with perspiration dotting his forehead and a frown on his face, he was the most handsome man she'd ever seen. And he was her husband. At least for two more days.

"Why don't you get in and cool off, sexy?"

"I can't." He moved to the edge of the pool, knelt and looked into her eyes. A mixture of sadness and hunger darkened his expression, and fear slammed into her stomach so hard she clutched her abdomen.

"Why are you looking at me like that, Brady?"

"I…" He paused and pulled an envelope from his pocket, his voice gruff. "I wrote you a letter."

Hope skittered through her. They had always communicated so well on paper.

But hope died when he placed the envelope on the cold tile beside the pool, gave her one last hungry look, then turned and walked away. Her hands trembled as she climbed from the water, wrapped a towel around herself and sat on one of the lounge chairs to read it.

Seconds later, the words blurred as tears ran down her face, mingling with the pool water. Damn Brady! In spite of their marriage, the priceless moments they'd shared the night before, in spite of their talk and her promise not to give up on him, he had just written her a goodbye letter.

"I'm sorry, Ali. I didn't mean to hurt you, but it has to be this way."

She'd thought he had left, but no, he'd stood in the background, watching her read his letter. He'd moved up behind her, so close she could feel the heat radiating from his body, could smell his intoxicating scent.

"Well, you did hurt me. Twice now." Suddenly tired and furious, she stood and swung around. "I don't understand, Brady. Why the invitation?"

His eyes narrowed. "What invitation?"

"Vivi showed it to me. The one printed with our names on it. I thought…I thought you wanted us to renew our vows at Vivica's wedding." The admission made her voice waver.

Brady looked stricken. He ran a hand through his hair, then scrubbed it over his face. "Jesus, Ali. That was a mistake. A misprint. I never meant for anyone to see it."

A mistake. He'd never meant for anyone to see it—meaning he had never planned on canceling the divorce and staying married to her, or renewing their vows. Pain so intense she thought she might collapse from it burned through her chest, all the way to her throat. She felt like the worst kind of fool.

Suddenly wanting to lash out at him for getting up her hopes, for coming back into her life and ripping out her heart again, she grabbed him by the arm and shoved him into the water.

BRADY SURFACED from the bottom of the pool, sputtering chlorinated water. He treaded at the deep end and watched Alison stalk from the room, muttering beneath her breath. Shaking water from his head, he contemplated going after her, but decided there was nothing else to say. He'd been honest with her— what else could he do? God, he hated to hurt her, could barely stand to see the pain in her eyes. But prolonging their time together, no matter how much he wanted to hold on to her, would only hurt her more.

He swam to the edge and climbed out, grimacing when the elderly aerobics class strolled in, wearing skirted bathing suits and pulling on pink swim caps. A gray-haired woman in an orange suit elbowed her friend and pointed to him, starting a round of whispers and giggles. Apparently they'd witnessed the scene.

He threw up his hands, shrugged and tried to hold his head high as he left the room.

The rest of his day went downhill from there.

First Vivica made him promise to join her fiancé for a bachelor party that night. Then, during therapy, he told her about the letter, and he thought she was going to kill him.

"You gave her a kiss-off letter?" Vivica added an ankle weight to his leg, forcing him to work harder.

Brady glanced up from the exercise mat. Vivica was standing over him with a fierce scowl on her face. Making matters worse, his insides were shaking with the effort of the workout. "I wouldn't call it that."

"Why not? That's exactly what it was, wasn't it?"

Brady slowly lifted his leg, gritting his teeth. "I was simply being honest, Vivi."

She put pressure against his upper thigh, adding to the strain. "So you're going to let this divorce go through?"

"Yes."

Vivica released his leg and stepped back, exhaling with such an intensity she sent her bangs flying upward. "You know, Brady, I think your leg wasn't the only thing hurt in that accident. I think you suffered brain damage."

Brady glared at her.

She tossed a towel at him, slapping him in the face with it. "Either that or you've turned into a coward."

"HANNAH, thanks for helping me give this shower for Vivica," Alison exclaimed. "I can't believe Mimi drove up to see Grammy Rose when she's due in two weeks."

"Me, neither," Hannah said, stirring club soda into the fruit punch. "I begged her not to go, but you know how impulsive she is. She said she had to see Grammy before the baby came."

"She'd better not overdo it and go into labor. The day's going to be hard enough. I'm counting on her to cater Vivica's reception."

Hannah circled her arm around Alison's shoulders. "Are you okay, sis? You look a little—" she pulled back and studied Alison's face "—frazzled and upset."

Alison turned away and placed the paper products on the table, half smiling, half crying at the sight of the wedding bells on the plates. She'd been fighting tears all day. Ten minutes before her guests arrived wouldn't be the time to let them loose. "I'm fine, but you know it's always crazy right before a wedding. There's a million and one things to do.''

Hannah set a tray of hors d'oeuvres on the lace tablecloth. ''What's going on with you and Brady?''

Afraid her emotions would show, Alison refused to look at her sister. ''Nothing. He's leaving after the wedding.''

''Oh.'' Hannah's voice echoed with sympathy. ''I'm sorry, Ali.''

Alison shrugged. ''It's okay, I just have to accept that he won't be a part of my life, ever.''

''You want to talk about it?''

The doorbell rang and Alison shook her head. ''Not right now. Maybe later.''

Hannah nodded. ''I've got all night, Ali. Jake had to go to Atlanta to testify in a homicide case he worked last year.''

''Good, then you can spend the night.'' *And I can cry on your shoulder when the party's over.*

''THIS IS GREAT,'' Vivica's fiancé said as a scantily clad waitress delivered a pitcher of beer to the table.

Joe's friends, two yuppie-looking city slickers named Curt and Dave, and Thomas, Alison's *boyfriend* and Joe's best man, grabbed mugs. ''Let's drink to our buddy, the first one to tie the noose around his neck,'' Curt said.

Joe laughed. ''I can't believe I'm doing it myself.''

Curt and Dave dragged fingers across their necks in a slashing gesture and roared with laughter.

Curt, a sales rep, whistled. ''You won't find me getting the old ball and chain anytime soon.''

"Me, neither." Dave, an architect who worked with Joe, pulled out a cigar and lit up.

"No way I'd give up nights like this," Curt said.

"Hey, who says you have to forfeit a little fun?" Dave elbowed Joe. "Right, bud?"

Joe shrugged good-naturedly, sipped his beer and laughed.

Brady frowned and raised his glass, feeling protective of his sister as Joe's gaze strayed to the semi-nude dancers twirling tassels and gyrating around metal poles in the center of the neon-lit stage.

"Now, take that one in the pink G-string," Dave said. "Don't think I've ever seen such a fine babe." Curt made a crude gesture with his hands.

Brady glowered and sank lower in his chair. Maybe he'd missed this stage of manhood or something, but nothing about the women appealed to him. Not their heavily made up faces, or their skimpy outfits or their big fake boobs.

He'd choose a night at home with a sexy woman who loved him anytime over some strange bimbo. He grimaced in disgust, his mind imagining such a night with Alison as his wife. Would he ever stop thinking about her?

"Hey, I'd rather have a nice woman waiting for me at home," Thomas said, mirroring Brady's thoughts.

Joe grinned. "Like Alison Hartwell, huh?"

Thomas nodded. "Yeah, man, thanks for hooking me up with her."

Brady crushed the napkin in his hand and saw red. Could he really give up Alison?

ALISON SMILED in spite of her misery. Vivica seemed to be having a good time and so did her guests.

"I love it!" Vivica held up a long black peignoir set. "You certainly know my tastes, Hannah."

"She knows what her own husband likes," Alison said.

Hannah blushed. "What did you expect from a newlywed—a toaster oven?"

The girls all laughed, and Alison realized how much Jake had loosened up her oldest sister. Hannah glowed with happiness.

Her cousin scooted over next to her. "Actually, I bought her the toaster oven," Rebecca whispered.

Alison chuckled. "She'll love it, Bec. Everyone needs a toaster oven."

Rebecca smiled and pushed her wire-rimmed glasses up her nose. "You're so nice, Alison."

Alison's heart squeezed for her shy cousin. Rebecca was beautiful and kindhearted, but she didn't seem to have a clue as to her feminine appeal. What had happened to make her cousin so lacking in confidence?

Vivica opened another gift. "Oh, Ali. The crystal frame I wanted for my wedding photo. It's perfect." Vivica pressed it to her chest, rose from the sofa and hugged her. "Thank you so much."

"I can't wait to see it on your mantel."

Vivica wiped a tear from her eye, then carefully rewrapped the delicate frame and reached for a gift wrapped in gold foil. Several of Vivica's co-workers at the hospital joined in oohing and aahing as she opened the remaining gifts.

"I love your shop, Alison," Rebecca said. "If I ever get married, I want you to help me plan my wedding."

"What do you mean, *if?* Of course you'll get married someday," Alison said. "You're beautiful and smart. You simply haven't found the right guy."

Rebecca blushed, letting her long blond hair spill over her shoulder. "I heard you and that doctor were going together. Are wedding bells going to be ringing for the two of you?"

"Not now, Rebecca. I need some time." Alison had just raised her punch cup for a sip, but paused.

"Really?" Her cousin's brown eyes widened beneath her glasses. "I thought...well, you know, that you two were an item."

"We've been dating," Alison hedged, "but I'm too busy at work to think about romance right now." *Because I've been stubbornly and stupidly in love with my husband.*

The doorbell rang, and Alison put her plate on the coffee table, wondering who it could be. She scooted between the women and hurried to answer it.

"We have a singing telegram for a Miss Vivica Broussard."

Alison gaped at the man in her doorway; he was over six feet tall and looked like a Viking, literally. He was dressed in a teeny gold costume and had long blond hair to his waist.

"Who sent you?"

The man raised a small piece of paper. "Mimi Broadhurst."

Alison laughed and ushered him in. "Hey, Vivica, I think you have another gift here."

Sixteen pairs of female eyes swung to the man, a mixture of reactions following: Laughter, shock, a few breathy sighs.

"This is your gift from Mimi," Alison said.

The man sauntered in, placed a portable CD player on the table, punched a button and began to dance.

Catcalls, whistles and laughter echoed around the room.

Alison stared at the man, thinking he was the most perfect specimen of human male flesh she had ever seen.

Unfortunately, he did nothing to stir her blood. In fact, she was more miserable than ever.

Because he wasn't Brady.

BRADY WAS MISERABLE.

By midnight, Curt and Dave were drunk, but much to Brady's relief, Joe seemed to be taking it slow.

Thomas remained sober, saying he was on call. Basically, the OB-GYN was responsible, mature and a genuinely likable guy. The sort of guy women liked and wanted to marry.

Brady hated his guts—because Thomas wanted Alison.

A sexy redhead tossed her twin tassels off the stage, a chorus of loud male sounds reverberating as some lucky guy caught them. Brady looked away.

He'd seen a half-dozen women in various states of dress and undress tonight, had even noticed two women at a table across the way making eyes at him, but he couldn't care less.

The only woman he wanted to see naked was Alison.

And that wasn't going to happen because he had told her goodbye today. Tomorrow he'd see her at the rehearsal, the next day at the wedding. Then their divorce would be final and he'd go back in the service for his evaluation.

End of story.

"How about a lap dance?" Curt elbowed Joe.

Joe shook his head. "I don't think so, man."

"What's the matter, afraid Vivica will get upset?"

"You going to let her keep you on a leash?" Dave asked.

Joe's eyebrows shot up. "I...no."

"Cut the guy some slack," Thomas interjected. "The man has a great-looking woman he'd rather wait on, right?"

Joe laughed. "Yeah, right."

"Come on, only two more nights of freedom," Dave said, pulling out a wad of cash.

"I gotta go, guys." Brady stood. "It was a good time."

Joe stood and shook his hand. "Thanks for coming, man."

Brady met his gaze, a serious warning in his eyes. "Yeah, looking forward to having you in the family."

Joe nodded. "Thanks. Me, too."

Then Brady leaned closer, his voice gruff. "You'd better not hurt my sister, man, or you'll answer to me."

Joe stared him down and nodded. Brady saw

Thomas watching him as he turned and walked away. For Vivica's sake, Brady prayed Joe behaved himself. At least one of the Broussards should end up happily married.

Chapter Eighteen

"I cannot believe it's raining!" Vivica darted into Alison's shop, shaking her umbrella, scattering raindrops everywhere.

Alison rose from her desk, dropped a towel on the wooden floor and mopped up the moisture. "I know. I'm so sorry, Vivi."

"It isn't your fault, but it's unbelievable. We've been having a drought for six weeks, and Mother Nature chooses the day of my wedding rehearsal to end it!"

Alison sighed. "Hey, look on the good side— maybe the rain'll stop by tomorrow, and the flowers outside will look even prettier."

Vivica flopped onto the love seat and slapped her hands down on the cushion. "I hope so. I had my heart set on that outdoor reception."

"It's always good to have a backup plan." Alison patted her arm, meeting her gaze. "At least everything else is on schedule."

"Oh, my gosh, you're upset over Brady, aren't you?"

Alison froze. She'd forgotten about her puffy,

swollen eyes. Even the cold compresses Mimi always recommended hadn't helped. "I... Brady wrote me a goodbye letter."

"He's an idiot." Vivica planted her hands on her hips. "But you aren't going to give up yet, are you, Ali?"

Alison forced a smile, coaxing Vivica to sit back down. "He said he was leaving, that he wasn't sure what he was going to do about the Air Force, then told me we were through. What else can I do? I have to have some pride."

Vivica balled her hands on her hips. "I'll have another talk with him."

"No, Vivi." Alison caught her before she could leave. "If Brady wants me, he has to decide that for himself. Besides, today and tomorrow are your special days. I don't want anything to spoil them."

Vivica's lips turned down. "Speaking of which, Joe didn't call this morning like he said he would."

"He made it into town, though, didn't he?"

"According to Brady, he went out with the guys last night."

"A bachelor party?" Alison couldn't help but wonder what Brady had been doing at the party. Celebrating his freedom?

"Yeah." Vivica worked the engagement ring up and down her finger. "I hope he's not getting cold feet."

Alison circled her arm around Vivica to console her. Of course, with the little she knew about men, she wasn't sure she could be of any help.

BRADY SPENT THE MORNING showing his mother's friend, Fred Fairbanks, how to operate the major equipment in the shop. Thankfully, the older man had experience preparing materials for presentations from his former company; Brady's mother had forgotten to mention the fact that the man had worked at a print shop in Atlanta for fifteen years. She'd also forgotten to mention that he had taken a personal interest in her. And if the way his mother kept blushing was any indication, she returned the feeling.

Brady was glad. His mother had been a good wife to his father, had grieved for him for years. Now she deserved some happiness, not to live the rest of her years in loneliness.

As he would probably do.

Plus, Mr. Fairbanks would be a great asset to the shop, and Brady could return to the Air Force without worrying about her. His mother had accepted the news that he would be leaving amazingly well.

He had spent most of the day trying to put Alison out of his mind. But he would see her at the rehearsal at seven o'clock.

The clock chimed five now. His mother had left early to dress for the rehearsal, and Fred had gone home to his remote control. Johnny and Bobby Raye strode through the door drenched to the core, despite the fact that they were wearing raincoats.

"Hey, man, wondered if you'd like to hit the Pug for a while," Johnny said.

Bobby Raye swiped water from his beard.

Brady hesitated, considering his options. He could kick back a few beers with them before the rehearsal. Then again, Vivi would kill him if he showed up drunk at the church. And he had to pick up Joe.

"No, thanks, guys, I have to drive Vivica's fiancé to the rehearsal tonight."

"Well, we'll be there later if you want to stop by," Johnny said.

Brady hesitated again, troubled when the men left. He had made the right decision about not returning to take over his father's business. He hoped he'd made the right decision about Alison.

ALISON MET Reverend Barnes at the front of the chapel. He was gray-haired, in his sixties and slightly hard-of-hearing, but everyone in Sugar Hill adored him.

"You're right on time, Reverend," Alison said. "I think the bride and groom are downstairs talking. They should be up any minute."

"You say you need a menu?"

Alison patted his hand, gesturing for him to turn up his hearing aid. "No, I said they'll be up in a *minute*." She glanced at her watch. "I'll go check on them."

"No, I don't need a check," the reverend said.

Alison chuckled and walked down the aisle of the chapel. She spotted Vivica and Brady's mother in the vestibule chatting with Donna and Tammy, friends of Vivica's from the hospital who were bridesmaids. Two young cousins—Priscilla, the flower girl, and Devon, the ring bearer—were there, too.

"I have them all under control," Mrs. Broussard

said. "I've been explaining how they should walk and carry themselves during the ceremony."

Alison nodded. "I'll get Vivica."

She rounded the corner to the bride's room, but loud voices echoed from inside, and she halted.

"Vivica, I don't care more about my job than you," Joe said, "but this project I'm working on is a million-dollar deal, and I had to call and check on it."

"Just like you had to stay out all night after that bachelor party. Exactly what happened last night, Joe?"

Alison closed her eyes, hoping Joe didn't have some horrid confession to make that might destroy Vivica's happiness.

"Nothing," Joe said, his voice edgy. "I had a little too much to drink and crashed at Curt's place. Don't you trust me, Vivi?"

Footsteps sounded behind her, and Alison opened her eyes and saw Brady descending the steps. Dressed in pleated chinos and a white shirt, he nearly took her breath away.

She had to get over him.

Vivica's voice broke the silence. "I do trust you, but I know how guys are when they get together."

"You know, if you're going to question everything I do, maybe we should rethink this marriage," Joe said.

Vivica's voice rose. "You want to call off the wedding?"

Brady sent her a panicked look and whispered, "What's going on?"

"They're having a squabble."

Brady winced. "Maybe we'd better try to pull things together."

"Right." She moved forward and knocked on the door. "Vivi, it's time to start the rehearsal."

The door swung open and Vivica appeared, her eyes slightly red from crying. "He wants to cancel the wedding."

"I never said that!" Joe exited in a rush. "Women! How does anyone understand them?"

Alison glanced at Brady for help.

"I'll go talk to him," Brady offered.

Alison nodded. "Vivi and I will be up in a minute."

As soon as the men left, Alison grabbed Vivica's hands and pulled her to the small Victorian settee in the corner. "Listen, Vivi, every bride gets nervous before the wedding. That's normal, so take a deep breath and try to relax."

"Relax? But what if he spends all his time at work and ignores me?"

"Has he ignored you while you've been dating?"

Vivica's chin wobbled. "No, but this week he's been gone and he didn't call—"

"Vivi, he's been swamped because he's trying to tie things up so you two can go away for your honeymoon." Alison handed Vivi a tissue. "Now, dry your eyes and let's practice your wedding before Reverend Barnes falls asleep in the pulpit."

BRADY SPENT TEN MINUTES coaxing Joe to calm down. "Look, man, did something happen last night?"

"No." Joe paced the tiny room. "I behaved myself, if that's what you're thinking caused this. But your sister has been a basket case lately. Complaining that I'm ignoring her when I have to work overtime. I was trying to get a bonus to take her on a nice honeymoon.''

Brady's respect went up a notch. "Listen, a wedding's the biggest day in a girl's life. They dream about it for years. I'm sure Vivi's just nervous. She wants everything to be perfect.''

Joe ran a hand over his hair. "Well, if she expects me to be perfect, she's going to be disappointed.''

Brady grasped Joe's shoulder and guided him toward the front of the church. "Just think, tomorrow night the ceremony will be over, you two will be on your honeymoon and everything will be great.''

Joe nodded and took his place. Dave and Curt, the ushers, filed in. Brady frowned when Thomas moved to the front to stand beside Joe. Jealousy balled in his stomach as he realized the implications: Thomas was the best man and would escort Alison down the aisle.

Brady took a deep breath. They would only be walking together—no big deal. It wasn't as if Thomas and Alison were getting married.

Not yet, anyway. *But Thomas wants her to marry him and it's just a matter of time before she agrees.*

Because you're getting ready to walk out of her life and leave her free.

ALISON SHUDDERED at the dark scowl on Brady's face as he approached them. She said a silent prayer Joe hadn't changed his mind about the wedding— and that Brady had changed his about the divorce.

But he passed her without a word, extended his arm and let Vivica take it.

The rest of the rehearsal was a disaster.

The pianist played the wrong music. The ring bearer chased the flower girl down the aisle, snatching her flowers. Donna tripped over her own feet and almost broke her nose. Tammy broke out in hives. And the preacher started the ceremony by reading a passage from a funeral service.

"Relax, everyone," Alison said calmly. "This is the reason we have rehearsals, so we can iron out all the details." She directed everyone to their places for another practice round.

The second time things went much smoother, except Mrs. Broussard burst into tears when the preacher asked who was giving Vivi away. It took Brady ten minutes to calm her.

"This is a bad omen, isn't it, Ali?" Vivica whispered.

"No, don't be silly. I've had much worse catastrophes happen and the wedding still came off."

"Like what?"

Alison struggled to think of something before Vivica panicked. "At Darma's wedding last month, the bride walked down the aisle with her dress caught in her panty hose."

Vivica giggled. "I'll kill you if you let me do that."

Alison laughed. "Don't worry, your wedding will go off without a hitch."

AN HOUR LATER Brady was exhausted from his mother's dramatics and the whole formality of the ceremony. And he was irritated as hell at the way Curt and Dave and Thomas kept eyeing Ali. Did she have to be so nice to everyone?

Dammit, she was *his* wife.

He felt like telling them so, ordering them to keep their eyes and hands off, but knew he didn't have the right.

The reverend summarized the ceremony. "Then I'll pronounce you man and wife and tell you to kiss the bride." The piano music started and the couple sailed down the aisle. Ali smiled and took Thomas's arm. Vivi's friend Donna walked down the aisle with Dave, a scratching Tammy with Curt.

Brady escorted his mother, gnawing at his cheek the entire way.

"Don't you think Thomas and Alison make a nice couple?" his mother said on the way to the restaurant for the rehearsal dinner. "I bet they'll be getting married next."

Brady drove like a maniac, imagining Emerson and Alison getting married, then imagining them doing all sorts of lurid things in Emerson's car. His irritation snowballed during the rehearsal dinner. Not only did Alison get sandwiched in by Curt and Dave and Thomas at the table—he'd thought the men were going to get in a fight over who would sit by her—but his sister kept singing her praises as if trying to pair her up with one of them.

"Ali has been great," Vivica said, beaming a smile at Curt and Dave. "Of course, we've been best friends since high school."

"That's right," Alison said, totally ignoring

Brady and enjoying the other men's attention. "We played softball together and—"

"Swam on the swim team," Vivi finished.

"I heard you were a great breaststroker," Joe said.

"She still is," Vivi interjected. "She swims every day at the rec center."

"Really?" Curt sipped his wine and angled his head to grin at her. "I swam in high school and college."

"You did?" Alison swiveled to study him. "Where did you swim?"

"Cal Berkeley. 'Fly's my best stroke. I'm more of a distance swimmer than a sprinter, too."

"Curt and I were on the team together at Berkeley, Ali," Thomas said.

Brady shifted and swallowed his bourbon. Dammit, no man called his wife Ali but him.

"Thomas was an awesome breaststroker," Curt said, gesturing toward Thomas. "We used to call him Speedo." They all laughed.

"You had to give up swimming for med school, didn't you?" Alison asked.

"Yeah, the schedule was just too much." Thomas placed a hand near her back, and Brady nearly lurched out of his seat. They had too damn much in common.

For the next fifteen minutes, they talked about sports, best times, Olympic trial cuts and different coaching techniques. Finally Dave joined in with a long story about a safari he'd taken to Africa and how he'd swum with crocodiles.

"Wow. I've always wanted to travel," Ali said.

"I thought you preferred small-town life," Brady cut in.

Ali's dark eyes narrowed. "People change when they grow up, don't they, Brady?" She turned back to Dave. "Where else have you been?"

Dave poured Alison another glass of wine. "Let's see, I spent some time in Australia…."

"Joe's friends certainly are interesting," Mrs. Broussard whispered.

Brady grunted.

"They seem like such nice young men, too. All with degrees and good jobs."

She wouldn't have thought they were so nice if she'd heard them at the bachelor party.

"And they seem awfully taken with Alison." His mother twittered. "She may have her choice of them to marry."

Brady chewed furiously as his future flashed in front of him: he was retired from pushing paper in the Air Force, still a bachelor, living at home with his mother. While Alison was happily married, with three or four kids, and had forgotten all about him.

Dammit, he didn't think he could stand it.

ALISON FELT HEAT scalding her neck as she and the rest of the wedding party rose to leave the restaurant. Brady had stared at her like a protective father— well, his look hadn't been totally fatherly—during the entire meal.

But darn it, he didn't want her, so she might as well try to move on with her life.

Not that any of the men, no matter how attentive

they'd been, had interested her beyond polite conversation.

She saw her mother and father pulling up to the restaurant.

"Thanks so much for everything, Ali." Vivica hugged her. The bridesmaids rushed away to get their beauty rest, but Curt and Dave lingered in the parking lot along with Brady, while Thomas went to get his car.

"Do you need a ride home?" Curt asked.

"I appreciate the offer," Alison said, "but Thomas is driving me."

"How about a nightcap somewhere?" Dave suggested.

"We could go to a club," Curt said hopefully.

Ali glanced at Brady, her stomach clenching at his brooding expression. Her parents were approaching, too, her father's hand resting on her mother's lower back.

"I'm going to call it a night, guys. I have a lot to do tomorrow before the wedding." She gestured toward her parents. "Besides, there are my folks. I want to speak to them. Good night."

The guys lumbered off, looking disappointed, but Brady remained, a sullen expression on his face.

"Janelle, Dad, what are you doing here?"

Her father clutched his lapels with his hands. "Your mom just bought a car from me, so I'm taking her to dinner."

Her mother gestured toward Brady. "I was going to call you two tonight, anyway."

"Oh?" Alison twisted her hands together.

"Something wrong?" Maybe the divorce couldn't go through for some reason.

"No, everything's on schedule. The divorce will be final tomorrow."

Alison fought a reaction, but the chicken Parmesan she'd eaten for dinner gurgled in her stomach. Brady stood ramrod straight with that military expression on his face. If they'd been at the pool, she'd have pushed him in again.

An odd look softened her mother's face. "You two do still want it, don't you?"

Alison hesitated.

She thought Brady hesitated.

But she sensed Brady was going to say yes, and she refused to beg or tell him about the technicality—he might think she'd purposely seduced him to make the agreement null and void—so she lifted her chin and strove for dignity. Then she nodded, said good-night and hurried to meet Thomas at his car.

Chapter Nineteen

Brady watched Alison leave with Emerson, a wave of anxiety knotting his stomach. He'd finally succeeded in convincing her they should get the divorce.

He should feel relieved.

Instead agony rippled through him.

"Brady?"

He didn't realize the Hartwells were still standing in the parking lot. Wiley Hartwell cast him a questioning look.

"So, I guess I was right four years ago," Alison's father finally said, pulling on his chin. "You're not the right man for my girl. She deserves someone who'd fight for her." Wiley shook his head in disdain and left him standing on the sidewalk.

Brady limped to his car, then drove out to the lake. Dammit, he was doing the best thing for Alison, wasn't he? He sat on the bank, pulled out one of Alison's letters from his pocket and began to read.

Dear Brady,

I've been writing you for months now and I don't understand why you won't write me back. I miss you so much. When I read your letters, I can hear your voice saying the words to me. But now I feel so empty inside and I ache to hear you just say my name. Please, Brady, write and tell me what's going on. I had a nightmare last night that you'd been hurt and you were gone forever, and I woke up crying. I don't think I could go on without you.

The memories we had were so wonderful, but they were too short. I want us to have more time together. I keep telling myself you're away on some secret mission, that you'll come back one day and my mailbox will be flooded. Or that I'll wake up one morning and see you standing in my bedroom.

I'm lying in bed now, Brady. Naked and hungry for you. I crave your touch so much, your kiss, your love. No man could ever take your place in my heart or my bed.

> I love you forever & ever & always,
> Alison

Brady crushed the letter in his hand, the words playing over in his mind. *No man could ever take your place in my heart or my bed.* But a vision of Alison and Thomas walking down the aisle hit him, and he wondered if another man had already stepped in to fill his shoes.

THE SOUND OF TORRENTIAL rains pounding on the roof woke Alison from a restless sleep. The flood-gates had opened, both inside and outside her house:

she'd cried all night long. She sat up, but groaned when pain shot through her head.

Even worse, the phone started ringing.

"I can't believe it's still raining!" Vivica wailed a second later. "What are we going to do?"

Alison pressed a hand over her eyes. "Calm down, Vivi. We're going to proceed with the wedding."

"But we can't have the reception outside!"

"I know." Alison carried the portable phone to the bathroom, wet a cloth to use as a compress, then swallowed two painkillers. Staggering back into the bedroom, she fell into bed once more. "But the downstairs will look lovely, Vivi. I'll make sure of it, okay?"

"Okay," Vivica mumbled. "I'll put my wedding gown in a plastic garbage bag to bring it in. What about the flowers?"

Alison stifled a laugh at the image of Vivica's five-hundred-dollar dress in a garbage bag, then flinched when thunder rent the air. "Believe me, the florist can deal with it. This is not the first wedding it's rained on, or the last."

"What about the food?"

"Mimi will handle the food, no problem." At least she hoped so. She wasn't sure Mimi had returned from Grammy Rose's, and Alison was worried about her pregnant sister driving in the rain. She'd make sure her father or Seth came to help Mimi.

Vivica sighed. "All right. I'd better call Joe and make sure he leaves early. I'd hate for him to get caught in one of those horrible accidents or a traffic jam on I-85 and be late.''

"Good idea.'' Alison hung up and dialed Mimi. Seth answered, his voice hysterical.

"What do you mean, she's not back?'' Alison asked, when he finally calmed down enough to sound coherent.

"She didn't come home last night, and the phones are out up in the mountains. I heard on the radio that Cherokee Creek has flooded and the bridge has washed out.''

"Oh, my gosh. Mimi can't possibly drive in a flood!''

"She'd better not.'' Seth's voice screeched with panic.

"Listen, Seth, I'm sure she's okay. Mimi wouldn't take any chances with the baby.'' Although they both knew how impulsive she could be.

"I'll keep trying her cell phone,'' Seth said.

"Okay, and please let me know if you talk to her.''

"Don't worry. I will.''

"Seth, do you know who she hired to help cater the wedding?''

"I think Rebecca might be helping.''

"Good, I'll call her and we'll make a backup plan for tonight.''

BRADY HAD NEVER SEEN his mother and sister in such a tizzy. Between hair and nail appointments, the phone ringing, the wailing about the weather and the frantic checking of last-minute details, he wondered if both of them wouldn't be psycho before they reached the church.

They were certainly driving him crazy.

His mother glanced in the mirror and shrieked. "Look what this weather is doing to my hair. It's so frizzy it looks like I stuck my hand into an electric socket!"

"Mother, it looks fine," Brady said.

"It's horrid." His mother grabbed her raincoat. "I have to run down to Thelma's and see if she can fix it."

Vivica rolled her eyes. "Well, hurry, Mother, we don't want to be late."

Brady watched them race around the kitchen, feeling tired just from witnessing their panic.

"Oh, my gosh!" Vivica squealed. "I broke a nail. I have to go see Deborah!"

He laughed as she tore out of the room, half-dressed. The phone pealed and Vivica yelled for him to get it.

"Hello."

"Brady?" Alison sounded disturbed. "Is Vivi there?"

"She just left, screaming about a broken nail."

"Oh. I just wanted to see how she was holding up."

"The house looks like a tornado hit it, my Mom and Vivi both need Valium, but other than that…" *I've been dying to hear your voice.*

Alison chuckled. "Then I won't tell her that the photographer just called in sick, something about being the victim of a practical joke in which he ate a chocolate cake made with Ex-Lax."

Brady laughed in spite of the tension between them. "So, there's no photographer?"

"Actually, I've already replaced him. We may have to pay a little more, since he's coming from Atlanta and he had to shuffle some appointments to fit us in, but he does quality work."

"I'm picking up the tab for the wedding, so don't worry about the cost. As long as he's good and he's on time."

"All right, well, let's just pray there are no more disasters today."

Brady agreed and reluctantly hung up, his heart clenching. Obviously Alison wasn't counting their divorce as a disaster.

ALISON'S HEART WAS racing. It was five-fifteen and Vivica hadn't shown up yet. The storm had worsened, dumping inches of rain on the town during the day. They also hadn't heard from Mimi. Worst of all, Brady hadn't changed his mind.

She supposed all the chaos should be taking her own mind off Brady, but she'd still thought of him at least every other minute of the day.

Now he was trying to settle Joe, who'd blustered in, saying he and Vivica had had another squabble. Brady and Joe were both standing by the door looking for Vivica.

Hannah darted over to Alison. "Dad just called again. Still no word on Mimi."

"How are Seth and Dad holding up?"

"Jake's with them now, trying to convince them they don't need to call the National Guard."

Alison forced a calming breath. "She has to be okay, she just has to be."

"Mimi may be impulsive, but she wouldn't do anything crazy like trying to drive in this weather," Hannah said. "She's very protective of this baby."

"She must know the roads are all washed out, too," Alison said. "Besides, Grammy would never let her drive at this point."

"You're right." Hannah chewed a thumbnail. "You don't think Grammy would try to drive in this storm?"

Alison exchanged a panicked look with her. "No way."

"Dad's trying to get through on the cell phones, but connections are out because of the storm."

The lights suddenly flickered off, and Alison thought she heard Reverend Barnes swear.

"I'll help light the candles," Hannah said.

Rebecca ran up from downstairs, hysterical. "Oh, my God, Ali, the lights went out and I ran into Thomas and just dumped a whole tray of pastries on him."

Alison grabbed her cousin's hands to calm her. "Shh, it's okay, Bec."

"But it was awful. I know he thinks I'm the biggest klutz in the world. And I ruined his shirt and—"

"Was he wearing his tux?"

"No…" Rebecca's voice broke. "But he's in the bathroom trying to get the whipped cream out of his hair, and now we're short on pastries."

Alison patted her back. "Listen, Bec, Mimi always makes extras, so don't worry. I'm sure there will be enough food. Is Thomas changing?''

Rebecca nodded, tears rolling down her cheeks.

Alison handed her a tissue. "Go freshen up. Thomas will be fine and everything will work out."

Rebecca nodded, blew her nose and darted down the aisle.

"Be careful, Bec, don't run into the—"

Her cousin slammed her foot into the corner of a pew and yelped.

The videographer tapped Alison on the back. "Miss Hartwell, without power, I'm not sure the lighting will be sufficient to video the ceremony."

"The electricity will come back on," Alison said, striving for a calm voice.

Mrs. Broussard rapped on the doorway. "Vivica's here! Hurry, Alison! She doesn't even have her makeup on!"

"How are you going to fix her face in the dark?" Donna asked.

"I'd probably stab my eyeballs with the mascara wand if I tried to put my makeup on now," Tammy said.

Alison felt her way down the aisle toward the rear of the church. "There's bound to be some flashlights here, somewhere. Come on, we'll manage." After all, they did have thirty whole minutes before the wedding began.

"The guests are starting to arrive!" someone shouted from the back.

Alison groaned. "All right, we need the ushers in place to seat people." She pointed to the piano player and directed her to sit. Hannah was helping the florist light candles along the altar.

Alison ran down the steps to help Vivica dress, praying she wouldn't break her neck. She might be getting a divorce today, but she was going to make sure Vivica got married.

"I'M NOT GETTING MARRIED," Vivica wailed.

"He'll be a great provider," Brady said.

"Rather a workaholic than a bum," Alison pointed out.

Vivica clutched the wedding dress to her chest. "But I'm not sure we should go ahead with the ceremony."

Brady paced the bride's room and glanced at Alison, then turned to Vivica, striving for patience. He'd finally coaxed Joe into agreeing to go through with the ceremony, but now Vivica was balking. "What exactly is the problem?"

"I called him to remind him to pick up his tux, and he put me on hold for thirty minutes and forgot all about me."

Alison bit her lip. "Look, Vivi, I'm sure he's just as frazzled as you are today."

"Yeah, sis, no guy's perfect."

Alison met Brady's gaze for a long, tension-filled second. "The important thing is whether you two love each other."

"She's right," Brady said.

"You're a fine one to be giving me advice." Vivica glared at Brady. "You love Alison but you're too stubborn to work things out."

Alison's face paled. Brady sucked in a sharp breath.

"This isn't about me and Brady, Vivi, this is about you and Joe," Alison said calmly. "You do love him, don't you?"

Vivica sniffed and nodded.

"Do you want me to get him so you two can talk?" Brady asked.

"No!" Alison and Vivica both said at once.

"It's bad luck for the bride to see the groom before the wedding," Alison added with a small smile.

As if they needed any more bad luck, Brady thought.

"Why don't you leave and let me help Vivi into her dress, Brady?" Alison handed Vivica a tissue. "Now, blow your nose and let's get that face repaired. Mimi taught me a few tricks about covering up puffy red eyes."

THE ELECTRICITY FLICKERED back on just as the wedding music began, and magically, the rain slackened to a light drizzle. Brady dimmed the lights to a soft glow so the candlelight bathed the room. Alison smiled, feeling a calmness settle inside the chapel. She watched in envy as the flower girl and bridesmaids strolled down the aisle.

Alison's dress swished softly at her sides as she followed them. Joe was beaming a smile, with Thomas grinning and poking him. A sharp pang squeezed Alison's chest. She wanted to be walking toward Brady, to be exchanging vows with him today, not ending their marriage.

Too bad he didn't want the same thing.

Tears blurred her eyes, but she struggled to contain them as she took her place, turned and watched Vivica and Brady move to the entryway.

The tempo of the music faded, and the wedding march began. As Brady and Vivica slowly walked down the aisle, Alison's gaze latched onto Brady. He stood tall, looking powerfully masculine in the black tux, and she couldn't help but remember the way he'd looked on their wedding night. Manly, but younger, happy and excited. Now he seemed solemn and intense, sad. Still, Alison soaked up his image, memorizing every detail.

She loved him more than she'd ever thought possible.

Thank goodness no one else knew about her hasty marriage. She didn't think she could bear the sympathetic looks from her sisters and the whispers behind her back when they learned of the divorce.

The next few minutes passed in a blur. The preacher asked who was giving Vivica away, and Brady said, "Her mother and I." Then he kissed Vivica's cheek and handed her to Joe.

The minute Vivica and Joe joined hands, the earlier tension between them faded and love replaced it. Alison knew they were going to be all right.

From the front pew where Brady sat with his mother, she felt his gaze on her through the ceremony. Unable to resist temptation, she angled her head so she could watch him out of the corner of her eye. When Vivica pledged her vows to Joe, Alison silently repeated the vows she'd made to Brady years ago.

She saw him twitch, then shift as if to stand, and

her heartbeat escalated. Was Brady going to change his mind?

BRADY ACHED TO TELL Alison how much he loved her.

Selfish or not, he couldn't stand to give her up. And what was it Joe had said? "I'm not perfect." Maybe Alison didn't expect him to be, either. He could accept his physical limitations, and maybe fight harder to fly again. He just knew he couldn't lose her.

"I now pronounce you man and wife. You may kiss the bride." Joe took Vivica in his arms for a kiss, and applause and laughter rang out. His mother started to sob.

Brady stood, ready to go to Alison, to declare his love, to ask if she could take an imperfect man.

But Wiley Hartwell burst into the church in a flurry of arms and legs. Seth and Mrs. Hartwell raced at Wiley's heels, looking shaken.

"Ali, Hannah, uh, excuse us, Reverend, folks," Wiley yelled out. "But we've got to do something right away. It's an emergency. Mimi's in labor!"

Chapter Twenty

"She's stuck on Pine Mountain," Seth said in a shaky voice.

"And Grammy Rose is going to have to deliver the baby if we don't hurry!" Mrs. Hartwell called.

A collective gasp reverberated through the room. Vivica and Joe both turned, grinning with joy, but concerned.

"I have to go to her," Hannah screeched. She and Jake started climbing over people, exiting the pew.

Wiley raced down the aisle, his lime-green jacket flapping. "I'm sorry for interrupting, Vivica, Inez, but this is an emergency."

Brady's mother clutched her chest. "Oh, my word, Brady, do something."

Alison stuffed Vivica's bridal bouquet back into her hands. "Congratulations, Vivi. Rebecca will take care of the reception. I have to go." She hurtled down the aisle, almost tripping, but Brady caught her.

Wiley yanked at Brady's arm. "You have to help us, son. All the roads are closed because of the flooding. We need someone to fly us up there to her."

"I'll get my medical kit from the car," Hannah said.

"I have to be there to see my baby born," Seth said, his face pale.

"You'll do it, won't you, Brady?" Janelle Hartwell asked.

Alison swallowed, emotions clogging her throat at the panic in Brady's eyes. She understood his fears, but she had to convince him to help them.

BRADY HAD NO IDEA what was happening, but he hated to leave his sister's wedding. And what if something went wrong? What if he froze behind the controls?

He couldn't put the Hartwells' lives in danger.

He broke out in a cold sweat, his pulse accelerating. But no one seemed to notice.

"Look, son," Wiley said, "don't let your divorce from Ali keep you from helping—"

"Divorce?" Hannah shrieked.

"Marriage?" Mrs. Broussard yelped.

"You're married to him?" Thomas asked.

Heated whispers bounced through the chapel like Ping-Pong balls.

Brady felt all eyes on him.

Alison wilted behind him and turned to Thomas. "I'm sorry, it's complicated," she whispered.

"When did you and Brady get married?" Hannah asked.

Brady's mother grabbed his sleeve. "Son, why didn't you tell me?"

"I...we can explain," Alison practically screeched.

Vivica hooked her arm in Brady's. "I'll fill everyone in. Go on, Brady. Do this for Alison."

Brady turned to Vivica. "But this is your wedding, sis. I don't want to spoil it."

She hugged him. "You won't, silly. If you help Ali, you'll make me happy. Besides, I'm married now, and—"

"And I'll take care of my wife," Joe said, slinging his arm around Vivica with a grin.

"It's time you took care of your own wife," Vivica whispered to her brother.

"You're married?" Thomas asked Alison again in an incredulous voice.

"So it's true?" Brady's mother fluttered a hand over her chest. "But then why was she with—"

"Mrs. Broussard, it's not how it seems," Alison said. "Thomas, please listen. I...it was a long time ago, in high school. Brady and I eloped—"

"And we thought Alison's father annulled the marriage," Brady interjected.

"I only found out when Brady came back," Alison whispered.

"We really need to go!" Wiley wiped a hand across his forehead.

Vivica hugged Brady. "Go on, Brady,"

Moisture filled Brady's eyes. "Congratulations, sis." He shook Joe's hand. "Glad to have you in the family."

Alison turned to Thomas. "I'm so sorry. It's a long story, but I thought it had been annulled...."

"It's okay," he said softly. He bent down and kissed her on the cheek. "Just be happy, Ali."

Alison muttered a heartfelt thanks, and Brady slipped his hand through hers, then smiled. Their gazes locked, a silent message flashing in his eyes— things weren't finished between them.

"Dad, did you know Alison was married?" Hannah asked.

"Yes, we'll explain in the car. Now come on." Wiley bolted down the aisle, leading the pack. "We have to hurry. Grammy Rose said Mimi's contractions are only minutes apart."

"Oh, Lord." Seth staggered.

Jake threw a beefy arm under Seth's shoulders to support him. "Come on, man, you gotta be brave for Mimi's sake."

"Don't worry, first babies take a long time," Mrs. Hartwell said.

"Do those breathing exercises like you and Mimi learned in Lamaze," Hannah instructed. "He-he-ho. He-he-ho."

Alison dragged Brady out of the church behind the Hartwell clan, joining the chorus breathing, "He-he-ho. He-he-ho."

When Wiley peeled the Suburban into the parking lot of the small airport, and everyone piled out, Alison stroked Brady's hand. Thankfully, the rain had eased to an almost nonexistent drizzle.

"When did you two get married?" Hannah asked, obviously still reeling from the news.

Alison explained briefly about the hasty marriage and annulment papers. "And Grammy Rose put them in my hope chest,'' she finished. ''So I asked Mom to file divorce papers.''

Hannah's eyes grew big, but Wiley cut in before she could comment. ''I called to see if any other pilots were available, but they couldn't find anyone.''

Brady squeezed Alison's hand so hard her fingers ached. ''Ali, I can't! What if—''

Alison pulled him into her arms. ''You can do it, Brady, I know you can.'' She cupped his face in her hands and forced him to look at her. ''Think about Mimi's little baby.''

Wiley ran ahead to check with George Frost about taking a plane. Seconds later, he returned, waving them on.

''I've got a Cessna 206 you can take,'' Frost said. ''Does *everyone* need to go?''

Alison's mother and father and Hannah and the others all stared at one another, then nodded. ''We Hartwells stick together,'' Wiley said.

George laughed. ''All right, there should be enough seats for all of you.''

Everyone hurried toward it. George approached Brady. ''I'll be glad to fly them.''

Brady met his gaze, Vivica's comment about taking care of his wife echoing in his head. ''No, I'll do it.''

Alison squeezed his arm, her smile radiant and confident. ''Thanks, Brady.''

''I'll help you get her ready,'' George said. ''I've already called about the weather. It's clearing up in the mountains, but the roads are completely washed away.''

George and Brady examined the exterior of the plane, then everyone climbed in and buckled up. Alison saw her father squeeze her mother's hand for reassurance. Jake was petting Hannah; Hannah was trying to console Seth. Brady gave Alison another pleading look, as if to say he wasn't sure he could fly, but she had enough confidence for both of them, and she intended for him to know it. She took the seat up front beside him.

Seth lowered his head between his knees. "What if we don't make it in time?"

"We will, man," Jake said.

"Breathe," Hannah instructed. "He-he-ho. He-he-ho."

The group chorused "he-he-ho" again as Brady took the controls.

BRADY BREATHED DEEPLY, trying to concentrate on the checklist, carefully scrutinizing each dial and gauge to make sure everything was functioning properly. His stomach balled into a knot, but he saw the love and trust in Alison's eyes and tried to push away his fears.

If ever he needed to come through for someone, it was now.

Maybe this was his chance to make up for all the horsing around he and Josh had done in the air. He silently reminded himself he'd flown through mock combat maneuvers, so surely he could fly this family to the mountains to see Mimi's baby being born.

Mimi... She was technically his sister-in-law. Meaning, technically, the baby was his niece or nephew. Brady couldn't let his new family down.

Alison reached out, cupped his face in her hands and kissed him. "I love you, Brady Broussard, I've always loved you and I always will." She gestured toward the controls. "Now, take me up like you promised me in your letters."

Brady smiled, remembering the first time he'd written her from the Air Force. He'd promised her he'd fly her through the clouds, that they'd soar over the lake….

The airport was so small it didn't have a tower, so he picked up the radio and announced his takeoff on the open frequency. Then he eased from the taxiway to the runway. Alison winked at him, and they accelerated until they reached takeoff speed and lifted off.

The Hartwell clan cheered. Alison's face broke into a smile. Brady's stomach was tied in knots, his palms sweating, but he guided the plane over the mountains and watched the clouds roll above him, feeling exhilarated and happier than he had in a long time.

"OH, MY GOD, I can't believe you're here!" Mimi burst into tears the minute the Hartwell gang exploded into the bedroom. And explode they did.

Seth fell over his feet and landed flat on his face in the doorway. Wiley burst right past him, perspiration rolling down his face. "Mimi, honey, are you okay?"

Jake dragged Seth up by the collar and helped him to Mimi's side. Hannah darted over with her medical bag. Mrs. Hartwell tottered behind them, looking nervous and shaky, with her blouse untucked and half her chignon falling down her neck.

The only calm one of the bunch was Grammy Rose. ''Mercy me, what's all the fuss about? Y'all act like we haven't ever delivered a baby in this house.''

Alison laughed and pulled Brady through the door. She had a feeling he was still shaking from the flight. They'd had to land on a narrow strip of pasture that had cows sleeping hither and yon, the grass saturated with rain. Except for the couple of swearwords he'd muttered beneath his breath, he'd maneuvered the landing with skill and ease. Then they'd all climbed up the hill, their shoes and hose and socks soaked.

''Oww!'' Mimi clutched her abdomen as another contraction seized her.

Seth paled and clutched his own stomach. Hannah pushed him into a chair beside Mimi and commanded them both to breathe. ''He-he-ho. He-he-ho.''

The entire group joined in. Wiley bent over Mimi and swiped at the tears rolling down his cheeks. ''I love you, honey. You're doing great.''

''For goodness' sake,'' Grammy Rose said. ''Everyone settle down. We'll go in the living room and I'll make us some tea before you all hyperventilate and I have to get out the paper bags.''

Wiley patted Mimi's hair. ''Mimi, you need Daddy, you just holler, okay?''

Mimi nodded, her teeth clenched as she struggled with the contraction.

Grammy yanked Wiley's arm and forced him to

go to the den. Mrs. Hartwell bent and kissed Mimi's cheek. "I'm here if you need me now, honey."

"I'm fine," Mimi said brightly. "Seth's right here."

Seth looked completely green, but his head bobbed up and down, anyway.

"Call me if you need me to do CPR on Seth," Jake said with a wink toward Hannah.

"Do you need help, sis?" Alison asked, suddenly feeling panicky herself. What the heck did she know about babies? What if something went wrong?

"Do you want to fly her to the hospital?" Brady asked, his calm voice alleviating some of Alison's anxiety.

"Oww!" Mimi's eyes widened with the contraction. "I've got to push."

Hannah shook her head at Brady. "We don't have time."

"Come on, everyone out!" Grammy Rose pointed to the door with her cane.

Alison, Brady, Wiley, Mrs. Hartwell and Jake all followed Grammy Rose into the den.

Ten minutes later, Grammy had them settled with tea, had given Wiley and Jake a Scotch, and had just finished telling them about Alison's birth when a baby's cry rang from the bedroom.

Brady squeezed Alison's hand. He'd been so calm and comforting the last hour she'd nearly forgotten he was leaving her.

Seth burst into the room. "It's a girl!"

Her father jumped up and shouted, "Another baby girl!"

Alison's mother burst into tears. Brady cradled

Alison in his arms for a hug. Tears of joy and sadness trickled down Alison's cheeks. She was so happy for Mimi and Seth. Why couldn't she and Brady have a happy ending, too?

BRADY WIPED A TEAR from Alison's cheek, touched by the family's emotions.

"Everyone can come in now," Hannah said a few minutes later.

Alison's father bowed to Grammy Rose and ushered her in first, then he and her mother raced in. Alison and Brady and Jake filed into the bedroom behind them and formed a circle around the bed.

Mimi was sitting up, looking tired but radiant, her red hair piled on top of her head. She was cradling a beautiful baby in her arms. Seth had his arm wrapped protectively around Mimi, his gaze fastened on his little daughter.

"She's perfect," Mimi said in a shaky voice.

"She looks like her mother," Seth said proudly. "Look, she has auburn hair."

Mimi brushed her finger gently across the baby's forehead, indicating the mop of curls. "And she has Seth's strong chin."

Grammy Rose laid a gnarled hand on the baby's back and patted her gently. "I believe she's the first of many more Hartwell girls in this family."

Jake eyed Hannah with a wink and Hannah blushed.

Wiley stepped forward, swiped at tears rolling down his chubby cheeks and kissed Mimi's forehead. "I'm so proud of you, honey."

Mimi reached up and hugged him. "Do you want to hold her, Dad?"

Wiley's face broke into a smile. "Of course I do."

Everyone laughed as he awkwardly lifted the baby and angled her toward the family circle for everyone to see. Wiley nuzzled her rosy little cheek with his face. "You're lucky to have such a good mama and such wonderful aunts, you know that, honey? And if you ever need anything, you know you can come to your grandpa Wiley."

"You'll spoil her rotten, Dad," Hannah said with a grin.

Wiley rocked the baby back and forth. "That's what grandpas are for, isn't it, sugar?"

"What are you going to name her?" Alison asked.

Mimi clutched Seth's hand and they both smiled. "Well, I wanted to call her Wiley, but we decided to save that for our son's name."

Wiley slapped his cheek and grinned.

"So we decided on Margaret Rose," Mimi finished.

Seth traced a finger over the baby's cheek. "We're going to call her Maggie."

"That's beautiful," Hannah and Alison both said at once.

"But Margaret is my middle name," Mrs. Hartwell said in a whispery voice.

Mimi nodded. "I know."

Mrs. Hartwell began sobbing. "I can't believe it. You're naming her after me?"

"I want her to know her grandmother and her

great-grandmother," Mimi said softly. "And to always appreciate how special families are."

"But I don't deserve it," Mrs. Hartwell said. "I was such a horrible mother. I don't blame you girls for not wanting me around. I neglected you all those years."

The girls exchanged sad but hopeful looks.

"You can change that now," Wiley said, putting his arm around her. "You can be the best *grandmother* in Sugar Hill."

"Yeah, you can learn from Grammy Rose," Mimi said with a wink.

Grammy Rose giggled and hugged Mimi. "Oh, sweetie, you girls made being a grandmother easy."

Alison laid a hand on her mother's shoulder. "That's right, Mom. You're here now. That's all that matters."

Her mother's chin quivered. "Oh, Ali, you called me Mom."

Wiley placed the baby in Janelle's arms and she sat down on the bed beside Mimi. Hannah and Alison gathered beside them, each placing one hand on the baby's back as a sign that Margaret Rose would bring them all back together.

"Wait, don't move!" Grammy Rose yelled. She grabbed a camera from the dresser. "I have to get a picture—this is definitely a Kodak moment!"

Chapter Twenty-One

Alison felt a rush of emotions squeezing her throat. She'd never imagined her mother coming back into her life and staying.

She'd never imagined Brady coming back into her life and leaving.

"I say we all have a toast." Wiley gestured to Grammy Rose. "You wouldn't happen to have some wine or champagne around, would you?"

Grammy Rose chuckled. "I surely would. Had a couple bottles left from Mimi's wedding." She hobbled off to get them, and Hannah rushed to help her. A few seconds later, they returned with filled glasses and passed them around.

"Here's to Margaret Rose, the newest member of the Hartwell family," Wiley said.

"And to her mother," Seth said, planting a kiss on Mimi's cheek.

"And to her aunt Hannah, who helped bring her into the world," Mimi added.

"And to Brady, who flew us all here," Alison's father added.

"Oh, and I guess we should toast Alison and Brady."

"I think I missed something. What's going on?" Mimi asked with a grin.

"They're married," Hannah announced.

"This I have to hear," Mimi said.

Alison glanced at the clock and realized their divorce was final—unless the technicality was true.

Oblivious to her turmoil, her family clinked their glasses, then sipped heartily. Emotions overwhelmed her and she turned to leave, but bumped Brady, spilling champagne all over his jacket.

"Better take that off and put some cold water on the spot," Grammy Rose said.

Brady removed the jacket and Alison took it from him. "Here, I'll take care of it."

She carried it to the kitchen, tears glittering in her eyes.

Brady moved up behind her. "I can just have it dry-cleaned, Ali."

"Heavens, no, it's no big deal." She was ready to dab water on it when she felt something in the inside pocket. Not wanting to ruin whatever it was, she reached inside and pulled out several envelopes. Her eyes widened when she realized what they were.

Her letters.

A half dozen of the letters she'd written to Brady when he'd been away. He'd kept them with him, even after he'd told her he wanted the divorce.

"Ali?"

She saw him standing by the kitchen table, one hand in his pocket, his eyebrows furrowed. Afraid to hope, she raced to the front porch and stepped outside. The night sounds buzzed around her— crickets, frogs, birds, the sound of raindrops splashing onto the roof from trees overhead. The air smelled of rain and wet grass, and then Brady.

"Ali, are you okay?"

She whirled around, angry and hurt and aching for him. "You kept my letters with you?"

He nodded, his gaze intent.

"Why, Brady? If you were so sure we shouldn't be together, why didn't you throw them away?"

"I meant to," he said in a low voice. "I planned on it."

"But you didn't?"

He shook his head. "I couldn't."

"Why, Brady? If you could throw our love away, why couldn't you get rid of these?"

BRADY SAW THE HURT and confusion in Ali's face and knew he couldn't hurt her again. And he couldn't deny his feelings any longer.

"Because I love you."

Her mouth opened with a soft gasp.

"I've always loved you. Even if I'd thrown the letters away, I would have still loved you."

"But you said—"

"I didn't think I deserved you, not after what happened with Josh." He lowered his head, the guilt still on his face, his emotions raw. "I thought I could never fly again, that you deserved someone whole, that I'd never be that man again."

"You told Vivica that nobody was perfect, Brady. I didn't want you to fly for me. I wanted you to fly again because I knew it would make *you* happy."

He moved toward her. "I know. And you helped me do that, Ali. Today."

She started to turn away, to fight her feelings. But Brady lifted her chin and forced her to look into his eyes. "I'm so sorry I hurt you, that I pushed you away, but I was hurting so much."

"I understand about the guilt, Brady, I do. But loving someone means for better or worse. That was in our vows, and I meant them. If you didn't—"

"I did mean them, but my pride got in the way, and I couldn't accept the man I'd become."

"Oh, Brady. I love you and I want you any way I can have you."

Brady pulled her into his arms. "You still want me as your husband?"

Alison's face broke into a smile as she raised on tiptoe to kiss him. "Always, forever and ever."

The kiss seemed to last forever, but definitely not long enough. Alison curved her arms around his waist, clutching his sinewy muscles as he explored her mouth and gave her a taste of passion. When he finally broke the kiss, they were both breathless.

"Then I suppose we'd better talk to your mom."

Alison jerked his hand. "What if you change your mind again?"

He pulled her to a halt and cupped her face. "I'm never changing my mind, Ali."

Alison suddenly felt a presence, and glanced up to see most of her family peeking through the screen.

"Does this mean you two want to stay married?" her mother asked.

"Yes," they both said at once.

Her mother's smile faded. "I'm sorry, honey, but it's already official."

"We're divorced?" Brady said in a gruff voice.

Mrs. Hartwell nodded sadly. "That is, unless you were, um, together during the thirty-day waiting period."

Alison swayed as she glanced at Brady. If she told him she'd known about that detail, would he think she'd tricked him?

"You knew about that technicality?" he asked in a gruff voice, as if he'd seen her reaction.

Alison bit down on her lip, tempted to lie, but dishonesty was no way to start a marriage, so she nodded slowly. "Vivica mentioned it."

"Vivica." Instead of anger or distrust, a tender expression darkened his eyes. "I guess I owe my meddling sister, after all." He cupped Alison's chin in his big hand. "So you're still my wife, Ali?"

"Yes," she whispered, tears clogging her throat. "But I didn't do it to trick you, Brady."

He traced a finger along her cheek and she heard her family's footsteps and giggles fade as they left them. "Ahh, and I was hoping you wanted me so badly you'd do anything to keep me."

Alison smiled at his husky whisper. "Listen, Brady, I already swallowed my pride a dozen times."

He brushed a kiss across her lips. "Well, then, would you marry me again? Will you plan another wedding, Alison—our wedding this time? One we can share with our families?"

Excitement danced in Alison's chest as he kissed

her ear. "I don't know. Your sister's was pretty hectic."

"We'll make this one simple." Brady narrowed his eyes, then nipped at her earlobe. "And I'll make it worth it, I promise."

Alison looped her arms around his neck and leaned up to whisper in his ear. "All right, but only if we get married up here on the mountain, in the gazebo, like Hannah and Mimi."

Brady gently tucked a strand of hair behind her ear. "I don't care where we have the ceremony, just as long as it's the two of us standing together."

"I say we'd better seal this proposal with a kiss," Alison whispered.

Then Brady claimed his wife-to-be's mouth with a passionate kiss and a promise to love her forever.

Epilogue

Alison ran her thumb over her grandmother's wedding veil, smiling as she thought about the hope chest and how it had brought her back to Brady. Today she and Brady, her one and only love, would be married.

It had been the longest and shortest three months of her life.

Brady had left for the Air Force the day after Mimi's baby was born. As much as Alison had wanted to marry him immediately after his proposal, they'd decided to wait and have a traditional wedding at Christmas with all their family present. She'd spent the last few weeks planning her own wedding. But she'd missed Brady terribly, and some part of her had been afraid that today wouldn't come—that somehow she would lose Brady again. He had promised to write, and this time he'd kept his promise.

Hannah and Mimi bustled into her grandmother's attic, where she was getting dressed.

"Where's my flower girl, Maggie Rose?" Alison asked.

Mimi laughed. "Mom and Dad are fighting over who gets to hold her."

Alison laughed. Hannah raised the veil and helped her pin it into her hair.

"You look beautiful," Hannah said.

"Brady's a lucky man," Mimi added.

Alison hugged both her sisters. "No, I'm lucky. I have a wonderful family and I'm so happy you're all here this time."

Grammy Rose knocked on the door. "It's time!"

The girls laughed and hurried down the stairs, each taking her place on the velvet carpet their father had rolled out as an aisle. White chairs draped with bows and ribbons were situated around the gazebo, poinsettias decorated the railings and guitar music strummed in the background.

Mrs. Hartwell carried Maggie Rose down the aisle, taking her tiny hand and dropping rose petals as they went. Hannah and Mimi, Vivica and Rebecca—all bridesmaids—slowly followed. Alison took her father's arm and glanced at her friends seated around the gazebo, then slowly let her gaze find Brady.

His dark hair gleamed in the fading sunlight, his smile shining like a beacon of light, drawing her toward him. The wedding march began, and she and her father walked down the aisle. The next few minutes passed in a dreamlike blur as they exchanged rings.

Brady cleared his throat. "I wrote a few things down that I wanted to say." He unfolded a piece of paper, and Alison's heart thudded.

''Dear Alison,

When I was a young man, I met you and fell in love. I knew then that no other woman would ever fill my heart the way you did. And when we pledged our vows the first time in the chapel by the lake, I meant every word.

But I was young and naive. Distance and circumstances came between us, because I forgot something very important about those vows— they were *for better or worse*.

It's easy to keep those vows when things go well. But they mean nothing if you don't have the courage to fight for them when things get tough.''

Brady clasped her hand in his, brought her fingers to his lips and kissed them, then continued in a gruff voice.

''But you had that courage, Alison. You taught me what love and marriage are really all about.

I loved you when I was a young man, I love you more now, and I will love you even more in the days that follow.

Your husband, your friend, your lover,

forever, Brady.''

A tear trickled down Alison's cheek, but she wiped it away and clutched his hand to her bosom. ''I wrote you something, too, Brady.''

He smiled and she cleared her throat.

"Dear Brady,

The first time I married you I was young and naive, but so much in love my head was spinning with romantic notions and ideas of happily-ever-afters. Now my head is simply spinning with you.

You have taught me that love isn't always easy, but that without it, my life is empty. You are my lover, my friend, my hero, and no matter what you choose to do in life, no matter where you go or how far you fly away, my heart will always be with you.

I love you today, forever and always.

Your wife, forever, Alison."

Reverend Barnes sniffed and dabbed at his eyes with his handkerchief. "I say you should kiss the bride."

Applause rang out as Brady swept her into his arms for a kiss. Seconds later, family hugs and congratulations engulfed them.

Mr. Hartwell pounded Brady on the back. "Well, son, how long are you home for?"

Brady smiled and pulled Alison into his arms. "Forever."

Alison looked up into his face. "You didn't tell me what you decided."

"I'm going into the reserves." Brady shrugged. "I want to spend time with you now, to make a family."

"Will you be happy with that?" Alison asked softly.

Brady nodded, and they both realized the family

had gathered to hear his plans. "I've already talked to Hannah about starting the medical flight services. I spent the last three months taking lessons to fly the chopper."

Alison threw her sister a shocked look. "The little stinker, she didn't tell me."

Hannah laughed. "He made me promise."

"It'll be the best of both worlds," Brady said seriously. "I can use my flight skills and help people here, then be on call if I'm ever needed in the Air Force."

"Did y'all hear that?" Wiley called. "Brady's going to run the medical flight services."

Everyone cheered.

Wiley hooked a thumb around his tux lapel. "It sure will be nice having a pilot around. Listen, Brady, can I keep you on retainer to run some ads for me? I've got some great ideas for this winter, I'm thinking about a polar bear...."

LATER, when Alison and Brady had changed clothes for their getaway, Alison hugged each of her family members goodbye. Finally, she made her way to her grandmother. "Grammy Rose, you knew all along we were meant for each other, didn't you?" she asked.

"Why, of course, dear. I could see it in Brady's eyes."

Mimi popped up beside them, the baby in her arms. "Grammy, I saw another hope chest in your parlor. Don't tell me you're already starting one for Maggie Rose."

Grammy Rose laughed. "Well, yes, I am, but the one in the den is for your cousin Rebecca. And next, I believe, will be her sister, Suzanne."

Alison, Mimi and Hannah laughed. "Do you think we should warn them?" Mimi asked.

Alison shook her head. "No, let Grammy surprise them."

Brady walked up and curved his arm around Alison, nuzzling her neck. "Hey, Mrs. Broussard."

"Hey, Mr. Broussard." Alison leaned into him. "You know, Brady, now that I've married you twice, there's one thing you could do for me."

"Anything, sweetheart."

Alison turned in his arms. "How about a honeymoon?"

Brady laughed and pulled two tickets from inside his jacket pocket, then waved them in the air. "We leave at midnight."

Alison clutched his hand. "Then what are we waiting for? I say I should throw this bouquet so we can get started. After all, you did write me some pretty steamy letters while you were gone. Something about flying me to the moon?"

"Yeah." Brady kissed her neck, then nibbled at her ear. "And I wasn't talking about flying in a plane."

Coming in August from

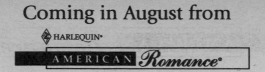

HARLEQUIN®

AMERICAN *Romance*®

and

Judy Christenberry

RANDALL PRIDE

HAR #885

She was the ultimate forbidden fruit. Surely now that lovely Elizabeth was engaged to another man, it was finally safe for Toby Randall to return home. But once he arrived, the rodeo star realized that his love for Elizabeth had only grown stronger and he'd let no man stand between them.

Don't miss this heartwarming addition to the series

Brides

for Brothers

Available wherever Harlequin books are sold.

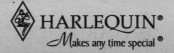

HARLEQUIN®

Makes any time special ®

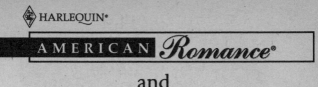
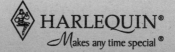

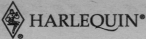

If you enjoyed what you just read,
then we've got an offer you can't resist!

Take 2 bestselling love stories FREE!
Plus get a FREE surprise gift!

Harlequin truly does make any time special.... This year we are celebrating weddings in style!

A Walk Down the Aisle
WEDDING CELEBRATION

To help us celebrate, we want you to tell us how wearing the Harlequin wedding gown will make your wedding day special. As the grand prize, Harlequin will offer one lucky bride the chance to **"Walk Down the Aisle" in the Harlequin wedding gown!**

There's more...

For her honeymoon, she and her groom will spend five nights at the **Hyatt Regency Maui.** As part of this five-night honeymoon at the hotel renowned for its romantic attractions, the couple will enjoy a candlelit dinner for two in Swan Court, a sunset sail on the hotel's catamaran, and duet spa treatments.

A HYATT RESORT AND SPA

Maui • Molokai • Lanai

To enter, please write, in, 250 words or less, how wearing the Harlequin wedding gown will make your wedding day special. The entry will be judged based on its emotionally compelling nature, its originality and creativity, and its sincerity. This contest is open to Canadian and U.S. residents only and to those who are 18 years of age and older. There is no purchase necessary to enter. Void where prohibited. See further contest rules attached. Please send your entry to:

Walk Down the Aisle Contest

In Canada	In U.S.A.
P.O. Box 637	P.O. Box 9076
Fort Erie, Ontario	3010 Walden Ave.
L2A 5X3	Buffalo, NY 14269-9076

You can also enter by visiting www.eHarlequin.com
Win the Harlequin wedding gown and the vacation of a lifetime!
The deadline for entries is October 1, 2001.

HARLEQUIN®
Makes any time special ®

PHWDACONT1